Between SIN AND SILENCE

WILLOW FOX

Published by Slow Burn Publishing

Cover Design by GetCovers

Edited by Marla VanHoy

Proofread by Ami K. and Jen S.

ONE

LUCA

I may have been an asshole, tossing Ashton out of the car during a surveillance op for my father, but I don't deserve what comes next.

In my attempt to head back down the mountainside, to find cover for the vehicle, I'm stopped by another oncoming car, coming head-on right at me, headlights blazing.

That wouldn't be the worst of it. The vehicle pushes forward, hard and fast on slick snow, forcing me to maneuver in reverse along the one-lane snow-covered road.

They give no indication of slowing down.

As I manage to make it through the swift turns in reverse, back up to the abandoned cabin, I have nowhere to go. There's no escape. Not even the cover of night will protect me.

There's also no sign of Ashton.

Desperate, I attempt to call Dante, but there's no signal. Not surprising. We're in the middle of nowhere.

Men flood out of the vehicle in front of me, blocking the road, guns drawn, its engine idle, with its headlights blinding me.

A darkened figure steps out. The man who was sitting behind the driver smokes a cigarette. It dangles from his lips as he lifts his right hand, giving a gesture for the men with guns to move in.

Two men whom I don't recognize come at my driver side door, smash open my car window, throw open my door, and yank me out, dragging me by my arms, letting my legs dangle on the cold, snowy road.

I'm entirely at their mercy.

"Get off me!" I shout, struggling against their grip,

fighting them off, kicking to free my legs and squirming in their grasp to break out of their hold.

Two additional men surround me with pointed and cocked guns.

Five men against one.

Me.

Who do they think I am?

“What do you want with me?” I pretend not to know what’s going on, but it’s not hard to play dumb when I don’t recognize these men. “I took a wrong turn. Look, I’m sorry! I’ll get back on the road, find my way to the resort. I swear I didn’t see anything.”

If only I can convince them that I don’t belong here, that I’m a tourist or here on a vacation to go skiing.

I’m not far from Blue Sky Resort.

They ignore my words.

I’m dragged inside the shack, an abandoned cabin, the ceiling barely stitched together, the place crumbling around us with broken floorboards at every step.

I'm just waiting to fall through the floor or get my leg stuck and broken.

The men put me on my knees. "Don't try anything stupid," the man on my right says. He's got a thick Italian accent and a scar protruding across his jaw.

Mafia.

He has to be part of another crime family, because he's not a Ricci and he's definitely not part of my father's organization.

I would know if he were one of us.

"Get up. Walk," the man grunts, the gun at my back as he pushes me farther inside to the top of the basement stairs. He hits the switch; the lights flicker before brightening up the stairwell.

It's an ugly fluorescent glow that hums to life.

"You have the wrong person," I say, trying again to reason with them. "I'm here to go skiing. I must have made a wrong turn because this clearly isn't the ski resort."

With a gun at my back, he pushes me to move faster.

I'm not even sure my weight on the stairs won't bring me tumbling down through the stairwell.

I pause for the briefest of seconds and I feel the hard metal reposition against the back of my head. "Don't try anything stupid," the man behind me urges.

Point made.

I continue down the creaky old stairs.

There's no handrail. The paint chips away at the walls.

This place looks abandoned, but clearly it has electricity. Someone is paying the bills. There's no sound of a generator, no sign that it's off grid.

It's being used for something far more sinister.

The floor of the basement interior is cement, crisp, clean, with a recent coat of paint.

That's not the only fresh scent permeating the air.

Bleach.

Which means they've likely murdered men down here. The fresh scent of cleaner burns my nostrils.

The second man who had thrust me from the car yanks a metal folding chair across the cement floor. The shrill sound sends a shiver down my spine.

There are cardboard boxes near the wall closest to the stairs, stacked waist high across the length of most of the room.

Storage and death.

A strange combination.

There's another door in the basement, sealed tight, with a padlock. I can only imagine what might be inside that room.

Another man, this one sports a hefty beard and long dark hair, a mix of black and gray. He throws my arms up at the sides and pats me down. If he's searching for a weapon, I'm not carrying one.

"Where's your phone?" his gruff voice asks. He doesn't have a hint of an accent. I'd guess he was raised around here, works for the man with the cigarettes, probably a soldier. He doesn't strike me as capo material.

"Not on me." I don't give him any more information

than he needs. It's in my car, which they can figure out on their own.

During his thorough pat down, he removes my wallet.

"I'd like that back!" I spin around to face him. I don't have a lot of money, but I don't need him stealing the cash that I do have on hand.

Although as robberies go, this doesn't exactly fit the typical stereotype. Besides, the mafia doesn't really care about stealing a man's wallet. They'd go after a small mom and pop store for a shakedown.

The bearded man opens my wallet and retrieves my driver's license, examining it closely.

"Luca Ricci." His voice is rough, and his gaze unapologetic. "Why do I know that name?" He brings my identification over to another member of his crew, the scarred man who dragged the chair for me to sit.

"As in *the* Don Ricci?" His accent weaves in and out, the slight Italian emphasis recognizable to the right ear. It's as though he's trying to hide it. His brow flinches as he stares at me, sizing me up, like he recognizes me.

It's not possible.

I'd know if he worked for Dante. I may not have been privy to all of my father's business dealings, but if he were a member of the family, I'd have seen him in the compound.

Perhaps they've crossed paths, but whatever's happened, whoever these men are, they're out for blood.

Hopefully, not *my* blood.

"Sit." The scarred man points with his gun, gesturing for me to put my ass in the chair.

"I'd prefer to stand." The longer I drag out every second, the more of a fighting chance I have of survival.

There's no sign of Ashton, which means he's my hope at escaping, or at the very least informing my father of our major fuck-up and my ass getting caught.

Dante will send his men to rescue me, won't he?

Unless Ashton opts not to tell him because he's pissed at me.

I did tell him to get the fuck out of my car, in the frigid cold.

Shit.

Plus, it's not like my cell phone was getting service up here. I doubt Ashton's is either, but maybe if he keeps trying, he can at least get a text sent out.

"As you wish." The scarred man smirks and then slips on brass knuckles before slamming his fist into my chest.

I swear my ribs crack, the pain radiating as I double over in agony, gasping for breath, and I collapse onto the chair, although I'm not exactly sitting.

The man yanks me up by my hair and puts me on my ass on the cold metal chair.

Heavy footfalls tread down the stairs. It's the man who was smoking the cigarette. His ashen hair and sullen face irk me like he's trying to figure me out.

"Seems we've managed to capture Luca Ricci," the scarred man tells the older gentleman with a smoke in his mouth.

He removes the cigarette, putting it out on the floor.

"Is that so?" He tilts his head, his gaze tight on me, and a crooked smile falls from his lips.

My heart races and my breath quickens.

I don't like that he knows my father. "Whatever bad blood there is between Dante and you, it's none of my business."

"You sneaking up to *my cabin* is my business." His tone is gruff as he steps closer and nods at the man who already beat me once to give me another lick.

It's like fire to the chest, making me cough and gasp as I try to catch my breath. I've been hit on the ice hundreds of times, plowed unsuspectingly, but nothing compares to the burn inside me right now.

Each breath scorches as I wheeze, trying to breathe. The pain radiates through me. "I wasn't sneaking," I rasp. "I got turned around, lost."

"A Ricci just happens to fall upon my cabin in the middle of the night?" The man tilts his head, bending down, his eyes level with mine. "Be straight with me and I can make this quick."

TWO

ASHTON

Luca had to be an asshole, toss me out of his car, right in front of the cabin where we were supposed to be surveilling the place.

My fingers are frozen. My jacket isn't nearly warm enough for this asinine weather.

Turns out, he saved my ass by kicking me out.

Am I ready to thank him?

Not quite.

Am I going to let the bastards beat the shit out of him a little longer?

Yes, but only because I don't have a great plan to take them all out.

I have one gun, but there are way more men, and while I've trained through the years, I haven't actually had any combat experience.

I grab my phone from my pocket. There's no reception. I wander deeper into the woods behind the cabin in hopes of gaining a signal.

My phone shows one bar and then nothing. I keep wandering, my footprints leaving an impression in the sludgy snow, and I walk the same path back toward the cabin.

I fire off a brief text to Dante.

Luca captured at cabin. Send reinforcements.

If these men don't find and kill me, Dante will when he discovers they've touched his son.

He's not a forgiving man.

There's no immediate response. The text shows that it's trying to send but fails.

Fuck me.

I have one weapon, a gun that Moreno handed me when Luca wasn't around. I might be able to take out one or two of the men, but there were at least four that I counted, or was it five? I can't be certain there aren't any additional men inside, either.

I creep closer to the cabin, and my phone buzzes.

I glance down at the screen lighting up.

Nova is calling me.

I answer in a whisper, "Can't talk now. I need you to call Dante. We're in some serious shit. He needs to send backup. Luca is in trouble."

Nova is barely audible, her words cut in and out as she answers me, "What. I. Can. Hear. Me?"

Which means she probably can't make out what I'm saying.

The call dies from lack of reception. I turn my phone on silent. I don't even want the vibration buzzing and alerting the bastards that I'm coming inside.

One last glance at my texts and the one to Dante finally sent.

At least there's hope.

I can't wait for his men to show up. Luca might be dead by the time they get here.

I cock the safety off my gun and quietly sneak inside the main cabin door, careful not to let the door creak as I slip into the darkened foyer.

The cabin is crumbling at every crevice, and there's no sign of Luca or the men who took him on the main floor. The cabin is one giant room, and then there's a door, left open, dim lights shining along the stairwell.

The light makes it easier to see the shredded floorboards at my feet, and I try to quietly hurry to the stairs.

The walls around the steps are crumbling, the stairs themselves look in rough shape, and they groan from my weight.

I wince and stop moving, praying that no one heard me.

"You think you're some tough guy because your father is Dante Ricci," a gruff voice echoes from downstairs.

Luca coughs. I'm certain it's him and at least I can breathe a sigh of relief that he's alive, for now. "He'll fucking kill you when he finds me down here."

I give Luca credit for not cowering or begging the man for mercy.

There's a dark, sinister laugh, and I quietly take the last of the steps, hiding behind the wall, doing my best to get an advantage on the men.

As soon as I take one of them out, the others will be on Luca in seconds.

Two men have guns in their hands, the metal glistening under the harsh lighting. The third man I can't quite see, but I hear him as he pounds the shit out of Luca.

Fuck.

"Is that all you've got?" Luca laughs darkly, and with his attention on them, I sneak down into the basement and find cover behind a stack of boxes.

I have to crouch to avoid being spotted and shuffle along the side of the wall between the boxes and the narrow path, trying to get a better view of Luca without the men spotting me.

He's hunched over, but his expression is emotionless.

Luca is well versed at hiding pain. But I know him, and I've seen that same expression on the ice when he pretends not to be suffering.

"Luca Ricci." The man standing a few feet away in a flashy suit seems to be in charge. He peruses his phone, which must have a signal via satellite, and smiles. "Congratulations are in order. I see you've recently wed and have a son."

My stomach drops at the mere mention of Harper and Zeke.

Luca takes a sharp breath, and I chance a glance at the two of them from around the boxes. I need Luca to recognize that I'm nearby if he's going to help me fight off these men.

"If you so much as touch a hair on their heads—" Luca growls and begins to stand from the chair.

He's not restrained, at least not physically.

The man who has been giving Luca a beating pulls back his fist. It glistens under the light: brass knuckles.

I lift my gun and take aim, firing off a shot at the man to Luca's right, one of them who holds a gun. The other gun is poised on me, and while I have the momentary advantage, they're just as quick, shooting two, no, three rounds at me.

Luca fights back, realizing that it's his chance at escape. He wrestles the man with the brass knuckles, slamming his forehead into the man's and knocking him momentarily off balance.

Another bullet whizzes by my head as I duck and am forced to follow the path around with one man shooting at me.

"Enough!" The man in charge lifts a hand to indicate for the carnage to end, but the other man doesn't put down his gun. "Come out. We won't kill you."

Doubtful.

"I don't take orders from you." I keep my gun poised and lift my head enough to take a shot, hitting him square in the chest.

The armed man releases a spray of bullets, but they're not anywhere close enough to hit me before he collapses onto the cement floor.

"You can come out of hiding. I have no need to kill you," the man says. "I'm unarmed."

I don't believe him.

I keep my gun poised and hurry around toward Luca as he stands. The man who was wearing brass knuckles lies unconscious on the floor.

Nice one.

"I suggest you move your ass out of the way, or you'll face my next bullet," I threaten.

He smiles, holding his hands up. "Tell your old man, Don DeLuca says hello."

The name doesn't ring a bell. Is it supposed to? "I doubt my father gives a rat's ass about you."

"Not your father. *His.*" He points at Luca.

"DeLuca?" Luca rasps and clears his throat. "Gino is dead. Has been for decades." He gets to his feet, quite a bit steadier than before.

"Not Gino. I'm not *that* old," he says and smiles darkly. "Massimo."

"Don't know any Massimo," Luca says, but the fact

he knows any DeLucas at all has me all the more curious.

“Listen, I’m all for reunions, but we’re leaving. You’re not going to stop us unless you want a bullet in your head.” I usher Luca toward the stairs as Massimo walks backward toward the boxes.

I can’t help but wonder if he’s hiding a weapon, waiting to shoot us from behind. I let Luca lead the way while I keep my back to Luca, facing Massimo, gun trained on him while we head for the stairs.

A handful of boxes topple over, the contents of red and black lingerie tumbling out onto the floor.

Luca’s breath catches in his throat. “You’re trafficking women.”

Don DeLuca grins as Luca stops at the bottom stair.

“Keep moving,” I mutter under my breath. Now isn’t the time for him to get all noble.

“Women. Children.” Don DeLuca tilts his head with a sinister smile. “How about I make you an offer? The wife or the son. Which will you give me and you both can have your freedom?”

Luca brushes past me, charging at Massimo.

I should have fucking shot Don DeLuca when I had the opportunity. He was unarmed. I'm not a murderer.

But now, Luca has him by the neck, blocking his chest, making a kill shot difficult without risking that I'll hit Ricci.

Massimo's eyes widen as he coughs and chokes, Luca's hands tightening around his throat.

Don DeLuca lands a brutal blow to Luca's chest, where his ribs have taken a repeated beating, and his grip immediately slacks.

Luca doubles over, and I take the shot, firing off several rounds.

Luca is gasping for breath, grimacing, and I know he just needs a minute to recover, but we don't have time.

"Get your ass up!" I grab him under the armpits, hoisting him to his feet.

He winces and groans.

"Upstairs. Now!" I shove him up the rickety staircase, and I skirt past Luca, opening the door, making sure we're not about to be surrounded by more of DeLuca's men.

There's groaning in the basement. Sounds of men stirring. There's at least one man who wasn't shot, and while I got several rounds off on Don DeLuca, I'm not sure I killed him. My aim wasn't what it should have been.

Adrenaline.

Anger.

Perhaps even a little bit of concern for Luca took precedence. I'll keep that little bit of information to myself. No sense in boosting Luca's ego.

"Get to the car." I usher Luca outside. The wind whips at my face and stings my cheeks.

Luca shivers, and I open the door for him, practically shoving him inside the vehicle. I'm worried that he's about to go into shock, or maybe he's already there.

Gunshots fire from the forest behind the cabin.

"Shit," I curse and duck, trying to avoid getting shot while hurrying to the driver's side of the car. There's broken glass on the seat, but I ignore it as I jump onto the seat. The keys are thankfully still in the ignition.

I put the car in drive and slam the gas. Their vehicle blocks the road, but I push it with Luca's car, tapping it once, twice, and then letting it roll down the mountain.

"Fuck, yeah!"

"My phone," Luca's voice is rough, coarse.

I focus on the road, heading down the snowy one-lane path, the same way we came up. "I don't know where your phone is. We'll get you a new one." It's certainly not the biggest priority. I reach into my jacket and shove my phone into Luca's hand. "Call Dante. He needs to know what we found."

Luca grumbles. "Still no signal. And my phone is on the floor, by your feet."

I glance down but don't try to reach for it. "Yeah, it's going to have to wait."

I'm already cutting the curves of the road too close with the snowy mess under the tires. The last thing I want is to risk us sliding off the road because I'm reaching at the floorboards for his phone.

"There should be a signal when we reach the main road at the bottom of the mountain."

Luca nods and wheezes.

I briefly glance at him. "You holding up okay?"

"Fine." He grimaces, and I know that look. He's in a hell of a lot of pain but trying to mask it.

"Do you need a hospital?" He's not bleeding out, but I suspect he has several broken ribs. I'm just hoping there aren't any other internal injuries.

"Don't you dare. Just drive me back to Dante's. I plan to have a few choice words with him."

"Like, who is Don DeLuca?"

He grumbles and shifts uncomfortably in the front seat. "For starters. DeLuca's my mother's maiden name. But no one ever mentioned a Massimo."

"Uncle? Brother? Cousin?" I start shooting off random guesses.

"I don't fucking know," Luca growls.

I'm cautious as we descend the mountain, keeping a lookout for any headlights coming up the road.

Nothing yet.

I'm not too concerned about traffic from the rear. We took care of that.

It's after midnight. I would have expected more cars up at the cabin, but when we showed up, they must have called them off. I did notice Don DeLuca on his phone.

Luca flips through my phone, the dial pad lighting up. "And he threatened my family."

I inhale sharply. I didn't miss the threat to Harper or to Zeke. Does he plan on calling Harper at this hour? He'd only worry her.

"Well, I shot him. He's dead."

"Is he?" Luca glances at me. "You didn't shoot him in the head. He was still breathing when we left him."

I slam on the brakes, and the car skids toward the edge of the road.

"Fuck, Rinaldi. Do I need to drive?"

"I've got it." I gently tap the gas. We're only about half-way down the steep road. "We can turn around. I can make sure that he isn't alive."

"We're not turning around. Not on this icy shit. Besides, do you remember being shot at when we were leaving?"

"Not something I can forget. Just trying to help. If he's not dead, we'll deal with him another day. Right now, we need to regroup and meet back up with Dante, let him know what the hell just went down."

"He may already know. I tried texting him, and Nova called."

"Nova?" Luca's head turns, and I can feel the heat of his anger radiating off him. "Why is my sister calling you during an op?"

"She was probably calling to wish me a goodnight. It's this thing we do, when we're not together." The smile she brings to my face just thinking about her vanishes under Luca's scrutiny. "I tried telling her that we needed her to call Dante, but I don't know that she heard any of it. I could hear like every fifth word when she spoke to me."

"That's sweet." His tone is fueled with sarcasm and disgust. "You having a romantic conversation with my little sister while I'm getting the crap kicked out of me."

"Nova called me," I reiterate. "Not that it matters anymore. We need to get ahold of your father, let him know we were ambushed, attacked, and that if they were intending to send reinforcements, to call them off."

"I'll get right on that, as soon as we have a signal." Luca is more than just a bit hostile.

I opt to ignore him. He's the one who got his ass dragged out of the car and beaten. He's allowed to be grumpy for one night.

THREE

NOVA

What the hell just happened?

I tried calling Ashton. Usually, we do a video call before bed, especially on Friday nights when he's done working with Dante.

It's almost midnight, and the call wouldn't connect to video. Audio was spotty. I could barely hear him, only a few words here and there. Nothing that made any sense.

I tried calling Luca.

No answer.

I'm pacing the length of the living room. Liam is glaring at me.

"Something is wrong." I feel it, deep inside of me.

Harper is already in bed, and while I'm worried about Luca, too, I don't want to wake her. She has Zeke, and she'll be up early with him in the morning.

Which leaves my only one option, telling Liam everything I know.

Which isn't much.

"I'm sure Ashton will call you back."

"That's what I thought twenty minutes ago. I'm worried. Should I call Dad?"

Liam shrugs and turns off the television. "Can't hurt."

Sighing, I rub my temples. He doesn't know about Ashton and me dating. That's the only thing holding me back from reaching out to him.

But what are my other options?

I dial Moreno, my father, and he doesn't immediately pick up.

When it goes to voicemail, I try again.

"I'm kind of busy right now," Dad finally answers, gruff and annoyed.

"Is Luca okay? He's not picking up, and when I tried Ashton, his phone cut out."

There's a silence that stretches on for far too long. "They'll be fine. Don't worry yourself, Nova. Goodnight." He hangs up without another word.

"He's hiding something!" I glance up at Liam. "You believe me. Don't you?"

"What exactly did you hear from Ashton?"

"I don't know. His words were jumbled. Broken apart. It's clear it was a bad signal, but I swear I heard him say something about Luca and trouble."

"Well, I mean, Luca and Ashton aren't exactly getting along. That's not news," Liam says.

His words aren't reassuring.

"Okay, but why hasn't he called me back? Dad clearly has a signal. Why doesn't Ashton?"

Liam shuts off the television and stands. "Do you

want me to drive you over to prove that everyone is fine?"

"Would you?" My eyes light up, and I'm already at the door grabbing my coat and slipping on my shoes.

He grumbles under his breath. "You owe me gas money."

We take his rust bucket of a car up to my parents' house. It's any wonder that the vehicle makes it all the way and doesn't bomb out on us. The car runs loudly, like everyone can hear us coming for miles.

The minute we pull up at the front gate, I give Liam the code and the wrought-iron gate opens. He drives us up to the front entrance, and I high-tail it out of the car, unlocking the door with my key, storming inside.

I slip out of my shoes, leaving my coat on the floor. "Just wait here." I glance at Liam over my shoulder and hurry up to Ashton's bedroom.

"Yeah, I'll just hang out here and look at the paintings on the wall," Liam says as he takes off his shoes.

There's no sense in announcing myself if Ashton is in his room and everything is fine.

But I'm worried that it's not.

Liam hangs back at my request, and I hurry to Ashton's room. I don't even bother knocking. I yank open the door, but the light is off, the bed is made, his bag on his bed.

I check Luca's bedroom next. Maybe they're hanging out, trying to sort through things after Luca found out Ashton and I were dating in secret.

I open Luca's door, no sign of him either. Light off. Bed made, and his bag is on his bed too.

I curse and hurry down the stairwell. "Dad! Ashton! Luca!" I'm hoping that one of them can answer what the hell is going on.

Dante steps out of his office. His eyes harden, and he flinches upon seeing me. "Nova, what are you doing here?" He looks from me to Liam, perplexed.

"Where's Ashton? I need to speak with him."

"He's not available at the moment. I'm sure you can understand," Dante says, forcing a smile.

“And my father?”

“Again, not available,” Dante says.

I step toward Dante. He may be a mafia boss, but he doesn’t scare me. “Listen, is Ashton in trouble? I have this horrible feeling that something bad is happening, and I just … I need to talk to him.”

Dante’s gaze flickers. “Why would you think that?”

I just told him it’s a *feeling*. Dante probably doesn’t get those. I don’t want to tell him about Ashton and me, because he might tell my father. But he’s staring at me like I’ve gone mad.

“I called him to ask him something about our assignment for Monday that’s due, and the conversation was broken apart. I could only hear a few words, but it just, it sounded really bad.”

Dante glances Liam over and then gestures for Halsey, who is coming down the stairs, to approach. “Take Liam to the study. Get him whatever he needs while I have a word with Nova, alone.”

Dante’s jaw tightens, and he ushers me into his office, closing the door abruptly behind me. “I need to know exactly what was said on that phone call.”

"Not much. I told you the call was messed up. Like the signal was bad and everything was broken apart when he was talking to me."

Dante sighs and leans against his desk, folding his arms across his chest. "What words did you hear?"

"I don't know."

"You have to remember something, or you wouldn't be here, concerned." Dante stares at me, and I shiver.

"I heard two words clearly. Luca and trouble."

Dante nods and steps away from me.

"Can you tell me what's going on? Are Luca and Ashton all right?"

"Sit." He gestures to the chair across from his desk.

I don't exactly feel like sitting, but I do as I'm told. My leg, however, bounces, seeming to have a mind of its own.

Dante steps around the desk, finding his own seat, his hands folded together as he places them on the desk.

"I'm not going to tell you what's going on because it isn't your concern. But I will say your father and my men are handling the situation. It would be best if you returned home tonight."

"Please," my voice catches in my throat, "you know something. I'm just ... I'm worried about Ashton and Luca."

Dante's gaze tightens. "As am I. And I don't need a teenage girl hanging around, causing me more grief."

I don't comment that I'm eighteen. While, yes, I'm still technically a teenager, I'm also an adult. That's not a fight that I'll win with Dante. "Sir, I'd like to stay the night. It's late, and my father wouldn't be pleased if Liam were to drive us back at this hour."

Dante is silent, considering my request.

"As a favor to your father, you may sleep upstairs for tonight. I expect you to show Liam to a guest room, and it would be wise for you not to come out again until morning."

"Of course, sir." I stand and rush to the door.

"Nova."

With my hand on the doorknob, I glance over my shoulder at Dante. "Yes?"

"If you remember anything else, it would behoove you to share those details with me."

"Of course. There really isn't anything more to share." I hurry out of the Don's office and catch up with Liam in the study, who is sipping a cup of tea.

"We're staying the night," I announce.

Halsey doesn't look pleased. "It's at Dante's insistence," I say, forcing a smile. "It's late, and he doesn't want us driving home at this hour."

"I'll show Liam to the guest room after he's done with his drink." I glare at Halsey, hoping he'll get the message that he's dismissed from babysitting duty.

Halsey nods and wanders off, which lets me breathe a sigh of relief.

"What's going on? What'd you find out?" Liam keeps his voice low. He glances past me and I take a look over my shoulder as another guard, Nico, walks the hallway.

"Not much. Dante wanted to know what I heard when Ashton called. He seems concerned, and the fact my father isn't home, and neither are Luca and Ashton—" I bite my bottom lip raw.

Liam smiles, but it's forced. "Hopefully, it's nothing. Just a misunderstanding."

"They're out on some mission Dante sent them on." I stand and wait for him to finish the last of his tea before leading him up to the second floor, where the guest rooms and my bedroom are housed.

Sighing as I approach the guest bedroom, I ask, "Would you mind hanging out with me, at least until Ashton gets back?"

"Sure," Liam nods. "Is this your room, or mine?"

"Yours, but you can come hang out in mine if you'd rather." I shrug.

"Yeah, show me your bedroom." Liam grimaces as soon as the words slip out. "Ashton is going to kill me. Unless, how about we hang out in his room? Do you know where he sleeps?"

Nodding, my eyes light up. "That's a great idea. Then we'll know he's home." I hurry to Ashton's bedroom and grab a seat on the bed.

Liam grabs Ashton's weekend bag, placing it on the dresser, making room for himself to share the bed with me.

I sit with my back against the wall.

Liam sits opposite me, stretching out while I sit with my legs tucked to my chest.

We keep the door shut, but the light is on. Anyone walking by would know we're hanging out in Ashton's room.

Dante didn't say we couldn't, he just said to stay upstairs, and what he really meant was leave him alone.

I'm following the rules, mostly.

Liam yawns and covers his mouth. "I'm not tired. I swear."

I snort but know he's lying. "It's okay. You can be tired. Just ... don't sleep."

"Gee, thanks." Liam smirks and rolls his neck. "Toss me a pillow."

I throw him one of Ashton's bed pillows, and he moves to his side, putting the pillow up under his head while he makes himself comfortable. "This is better."

"Ashton is going to have your head when he realizes the bed pillows smell like you."

"Oh, come on. He'll see me in here, with all my clothes on. Relax, he's not Luca." Liam doesn't so much as budge. He's comfortable, and I don't blame him for stretching out.

That garners a smile out of me. "He's definitely not Luca."

We share a smile and then a laugh.

"You know who I like. Tell me about the girl you like." I try to keep Liam awake, although he isn't exactly fighting sleep. He just looks super cozy stretched out.

Me? I'm a ticking time bomb. Worry floods all of my senses. Talking is at least a distraction.

"Bristol Greyson," Liam admits, and his cheeks redden. "I swear, I hated her up until that kiss. Have you ever kissed someone, and you craved more? Like one kiss isn't enough and you need more to survive?"

I chuckle. "You don't want to hear about Ashton's and my sex life. But I do want to know more about this fiery seductress who kisses like a goddess."

"Boy, does that ever describe her. Except I think you mean succubus."

I double over laughing, my legs sliding out to the side on the mattress. "Oh my gosh! She can't be that bad."

"She is. She punched me in the first grade." Liam stares at me, serious.

"I'll bet you deserved it."

His eyes narrow, and he thinks it over for a moment. "I may have been flirting with her."

"Wow. So, you've had a crush on her for over a decade."

He shoves me with his feet. "Don't go getting any ideas. I hated her for all of that time. I swear, it wasn't until that kiss and her shoving me out of her dorm room that I started catching feelings."

"What were you doing in her dorm room?" I need all the juicy details. If he hates her so much, how did they end up kissing?

"I went looking for Iris. Ended up on the wrong floor. Stupid mistake."

"And kissing Bristol?" I tilt my head, waiting to see if Liam also claims that was a mistake.

"Was the highlight of my year so far."

"It's only March. Have you tried reaching out to her?"

"And say what?" Liam's nose scrunches in disgust. "We have a salty history. If she liked kissing me, she wouldn't have shoved me out of her dorm room."

"Maybe the kiss surprised her as much as it surprised you?" I shuffle down on the bed but let the pillows prop me up. I hate to admit I love listening to all of Liam's dirty deeds, because he's one who usually doesn't kiss and tell.

I'm a girl for gossip.

"Maybe. I don't know."

He's clearly second-guessing himself or the kiss.

"Do you have her phone number? You could text her and suggest coffee. That's a pretty safe date."

"I'm not dating her, Nova."

"Well, obviously not yet." Grinning, I hold out my hand. "Give me your phone."

"Why?"

"Do you have her number or contact information?"

"She's on my social media."

My eyes light up. "Stalker." I'm joking with Liam, but he blushes again. So, he has been stalking her social media feed.

He pulls up her profile and slides his phone across the bed. "Don't comment or hit like on any of her posts."

"Right. You can't let her know that you actually like her." I shake my head and scroll through her wall. There are lots of photographs of her and her friends. There are also several of her at Ice Dragons' games, wearing their jersey and posing with different players. The pictures are posted over several years as I keep scrolling, even more of them when she was younger. The girl clearly has an "in" with the team. "She's cute."

"I know," Liam says, and his nose wrinkles with a wry grin.

"And she's single, according to her profile."

"Yeah, well, I'm not going to ask her out." Liam yanks the phone from my hand.

Pouting, I gesture for him to deposit the phone back into my hand. "You should send her a message, or I can do it, as you."

"You're not contacting her!" Liam scowls and then glances at his phone, staring at her photo, which is still on the screen. His eyes soften, as does the look on his face.

He's smitten.

"What if I reach out to her, as myself?" I suggest.

"How is that going to help? You're a stranger."

"I could tell her I'm a huge Ice Dragons' fan. My brother plays hockey, and I could ask if she might get him an autograph for his birthday? Since, clearly, she knows some of the players on the team." It's the first thought I have, and Liam laughs.

"Fuck, no. Please don't do that. You'll embarrass all of us, including Luca, and he will be pissed at you again."

"What? Why?" I don't understand why my suggestion is that terrible.

"Kyler Greyson isn't just *some* hockey player."

"Wait." My jaw drops at the mention of Kyler Greyson. "Her father is *the* Kyler Greyson? MVP. Star hockey player for the Ice Dragons. Now current owner?"

Liam silently nods.

"Oh, damn. Yeah, you're fucked."

"I know." Liam rolls onto his back and stares up at the ceiling. He brings his phone above his head, scrolling through more of her feed. "Fucked and horny."

I shove him with my feet. "Gross."

"Sorry, but it's true. She's hot. Have you seen her in a bikini?" Liam scrolls until he shows me one of her summer photos that she posted of her and the girls at the beach in California.

"She's cute. I get it."

"She's more than cute," Liam says, and I can hear the dreamy tone in his voice that has him head over heels for Bristol.

"Then grow a pair and call her."

I've never known Liam to be shy. He's certainly more reserved than Ashton and Luca, but shy, no.

"I don't have her phone number."

"That's just an excuse. You could send her a message, ask her for it."

"Also, no." Liam shoots down my suggestion.

"Show up at her dorm room?" If he's got it that bad for her, maybe she has the hots for him, too, and they could just fuck and get it out of their systems?

He has always been more about friends-with-benefits than relationships.

Liam is quiet as he considers my suggestion. "I'll need an excuse. A reason that I stopped by, without looking like I'm obsessed with her."

"But you are ... in a good way." From what I can tell, he isn't exhibiting stalker signs, except maybe staring at her social media profile for ungodly amounts of time.

"You're not helping," Liam grumbles. "A reason that I show up at her dorm room. And it can't be because I got the wrong room again."

"Why can't it?" I shrug and laugh. "Booty call. Or bring pizza," I suggest.

"What if she's not home? Or slams the door in my face?" Liam is already coming up with all the reasons it won't work.

"Both valid possibilities."

He groans and rolls back onto his side. "You're not helping."

"Oh, was I supposed to be? I mean, we could give you a fake girlfriend and see if she gets jealous, but since you said the girl hates you, I doubt that will work."

Liam snarls at me. "You're just being mean now."

"I'm not!" I laugh and grab his phone from his hands.

"Nova! Give that back." He reaches for the phone, and I keep it far from his grasp.

Liam climbs across the bed, leaning over me, his fingers attempting to pluck the phone from my death grip.

Ashton's tired and worn expression turns red. "What the hell is going on?"

"You're home!" My voice comes out more as a squeak than I intend. I release my grip on Liam's phone and shove him off me. "I was worried about you."

Ashton's gaze narrows. "Looks like you were *really* worried. What the hell are you doing here, Moretti?"

Liam clears his throat and shifts back on the bed, falling onto his ass. "Keeping your girlfriend company while we were waiting for you to get home."

"Great. I'm home. Now get the fuck out of my room," Ashton growls at Liam, and I smile apologetically.

"Thanks," I whisper to Liam as he brushes past Ashton, who is practically blocking the door.

The moment Liam is out of the bedroom, he shuts it briskly behind him, and a rush of wind hits me.

I breathe a sigh of relief as I glance over Ashton. There's no sign of a struggle. He looks all right, just tired and, pissed. "Hey," I say and smile. "You're okay."

"I'm just fucking peachy." He stalks to the dresser, stripping out of his clothes.

I inhale sharply, watching him disrobe.

His lines are taunt. His muscles ripple as he keeps his back to me. But I catch a glimpse of him in the reflection of the mirror and his eyes land on me.

He thrusts a pair of boxers into his palm and yanks them up, hiding himself from me.

Ashton turns around to face me, his eyes dark. There's no smile on his face. No hint of happiness that he's pleased I'm here. "If you're sleeping in my bed, then you'd better fucking get undressed."

I inhale sharply and quickly disrobe. He doesn't have to tell me twice to get naked. My clothes are thrown to the opposite side of the room, near the closed door.

"Is this better?" I ask, letting him ogle me.

He hits the light on the wall, basking the room in darkness as he approaches the bed. I sit up, reaching for him, finding his mouth, his tongue, his lips.

He takes my breath away, our kiss searing and

heated as he pushes me down on the mattress onto my back.

Each breath is heavy, loaded, fueled with need.

"Fuck," Ashton rasps, and he buries me beneath him, dragging my leg up around him as he grinds against me.

We're kissing, practically tongue fucking and I feel his hard-on poke me through his boxers.

My fingers roam down his chest, into his waistband, touching him, grazing him at first, feeling his body respond.

"I need you, Nova," his whispered words are pleas, and I nod.

Unsure if he can see me in the darkness, I kiss him and push at his boxers, helping him out of the only scrap of clothing between us.

"Take whatever you need from me, Ashton. I'm yours."

He growls, and his fingers swiftly enter me, teasing and coating my folds. "Fuck, you're already wet for me." He pauses, and silence fills the room. "Or is it..."

I silence him before he can even say that thought aloud.

Liam is nothing more than a friend.

Ashton is my everything.

"You make me like this—needy, raw, primal." I drag my lips across his and down his neck. "Fucking take me. I'm yours."

Within seconds, he grabs a condom, readjusts, and then he's inside me, stretching me.

"Fuck," I rasp, my neck falling back against the pillow, eyes shutting for a moment.

Heat floods all of my senses.

"You're so tight but feel so incredible," he whispers into my ear and then nips at my neck.

I yelp, and he pushes deeper, driving harder and faster. He pins me down, his hands pressing me against the bed as I wrap my legs around him, wanting more.

His mouth finds mine, silencing me, keeping anyone from overhearing the sounds I'm making as the bed creaks and groans beneath us.

The bedroom door flies open, and both of us catch a glance at Luca, who doesn't even have the decency to knock.

"Nova?" Luca's brow pinches, and he runs a hand through his hair.

"Who'd you think I was fucking?" Ashton bites out at his best friend.

Luca shakes his head and backs out, slamming the door shut.

"Shit," Ashton grumbles and rolls off me.

I inhale sharply and roll onto my side, dragging my leg over his. "Do you need to go check on him?"

"He decided to come in without knocking!" Ashton's breathing hard, trying to catch his breath.

Sweat trickles on my forehead. "We could just ignore it?" It's not like we haven't been interrupted before, this isn't anything new. Locking the bedroom door, however, should be an automatic by now.

Ashton glances at me and shakes his head. "I can't. Tonight was..." The words hang in the air.

"Do you want to talk about it?" I ask, offering to listen.

"You know I can't." Ashton's gaze winces, like he's thinking over the night's events.

I run my fingers over his chest to try to settle him down. "You know nothing between Liam and I—"

"I know," Ashton says and sighs. "He just made me see red when I came in, expecting to get some rest, and then you're on my bed with *him*."

"It's Liam," I say, smiling. "Come on."

"Yeah, well, *we* were just friends once too."

I pinch him on the arm for that comment.

"Ow." He grimaces, and I roll my eyes.

There's no way I hurt him, other than perhaps his pride. "You and I are more than friends." I climb onto him, straddling his hips, staring down at him. My hair curtains around us, the world disappearing. "Don't even suggest that I would do anything with Liam again."

"Fine," Ashton says and sighs. His hands find my hips, his fingers dancing over my skin. "What are you doing here tonight? What are you both doing here?"

"I was worried when you called and I couldn't quite understand your message. I tried calling Dad, but he practically hung up on me. So, I convinced Liam to drive us here so I could make sure you were safe."

"Us? Are Harper and Zeke here too?"

I shake my head and drop a kiss on his lips. He doesn't kiss me back. His body is tense.

"No, she's still at home, asleep. Why do you have that look on your face?"

FOUR

LUCA

I can't sleep. Between witnessing my best friend and little sister fornicating like wild beasts and the pain throbbing in my chest like nothing I've ever felt before, I'm not even tired.

The assault leaves me with fresh bruises, my skin marked by those damn brass knuckles, and when I take a deep breath, it stabs viciously within me. I've had my ass beaten enough times on the ice to leave welts, but they're nothing close to the sensation I feel now.

But I'm always wearing protective gear when I'm playing hockey.

Can't say I was lucky enough to suit up before getting my ass beaten tonight.

I grumble as I climb out of bed, an uncomfortable feat that drags me out of my room.

The house is dark, but there's always someone awake, keeping watch over the compound.

I barely spoke two words to my father when I came home. I blasted him with my middle finger and stormed to my room.

It's like reliving my childhood or, rather, my teenager years all over again.

I head down the stairs. If Harper were here, I'd have climbed into her bed. At least her warmth might have brought me comfort to dull the throbbing sensations in my chest.

Instead, I'm left alone.

It's for the best; her and Zeke under my father's roof isn't the best idea.

And yet, Massimo's words reverberate through my mind.

He threatened my family.

I stalk past Dante's office and pause.

He either left the light on or he's still awake at this awful hour.

I don't bother to knock. If it's another one of his men in his office, I'll see what trouble they're up to.

I storm inside, and Dante glances up with a heavy gaze from his laptop.

His eyes tighten, and he gestures to the seat across from his desk. "You're awake."

I shut the door behind myself and find my way to the leather chair. It's cool against my skin. I feel a bit underdressed. My father, always in a suit. Me, in my boxers and a t-shirt. Mostly the t-shirt is so I don't have to stare at the unsightly bruises forming on my chest when I look in the mirror. While it may not be often, it's often enough.

"Who is Massimo DeLuca?" I ask.

Dante emits a heavy sigh, pushes his chair backward and stands. He approaches his liquor tray against the far wall. Pouring himself a scotch, he grabs a few cubes from the ice bucket beside the liquor.

“I’m sure you recognize the DeLuca surname.” Dante swirls the liquor and breathes it in before sampling it.

“It’s Mom’s maiden name.”

Dante nods, his face a scowl as he’s wrapped up in his head for a moment. “Massimo is a name I haven’t heard in quite a long time.”

I open my mouth to ask again who the hell Massimo is when Dante finally answers, “He’s your uncle. Your mother had an older brother whom she is estranged from.”

Mom is estranged from her entire family, but no one had ever mentioned that she had a sibling. “She never speaks about him.”

“He’s as ruthless and cunning as Gino was, and I’m guessing he’s taken over the family business.”

I snort in disgust. Standing, I help myself to my father’s scotch.

He raises an eyebrow at me. “Aren’t you a little young to be drinking?”

“Comes with the cost of you and I doing business together. Any more family secrets?” I pour myself a glass and breathe in the aroma. My nostrils already burn, and I haven't yet tasted it.

I take a gulp and wince.

It's like turpentine.

"You sip scotch, not throw it back like a shot," he scolds.

"My mistake." I pour another glass because, fuck it if Dante is going to tell me how to drink liquor.

He raises an eyebrow at me but doesn't comment on my underage drinking again. Good, because there's not a lot he can say that will save him tonight.

"Do you want to tell me what exactly went down this evening?" Dante swirls the amber liquid and glances at me, his gaze filled with something I don't quite recognize.

Concern.

"I got yanked out of my car, dragged inside, beaten, and learned I have an uncle. Does that about sum it all up for you?" My tone is harsh and bitter, and I swallow back another gulp of the ridiculously expensive scotch. Knowing my father, he dropped a solid five figures on the bottle.

Dante nods slowly. "The only part I'm not quite comprehending is how Ashton managed not to get taken when you did."

I inhale sharply and wince.

Fuck, that hurts.

Dante notices my grimace, and he stands, coming to tower over me. "Did Massimo do something to hurt you?"

I clear my throat.

I don't need Dante's pity.

"I'm fine." My ribs and chest scream otherwise at me, causing a slight headache, but at least I know there's no concussion since I didn't hit my head. Score one for Team Luca.

"You look fine, clearly." Dante smirks, not the least bit convinced. "Do I need to send in the physician?"

"That isn't necessary." I meet my old man's stare. The only way out of *this* line of questioning is by telling him about the spat Ashton and I had, which isn't going to please him.

"Good. I'd hate to think a DeLuca laid hands on my son."

I huff under my breath and wince.

Fucking pain.

Dante's head tilts, convinced that I'm hiding something, and he reaches for his cell phone on the desk.

"Ashton and I were arguing when we arrived at the cabin." I hate myself for giving Dante any of the details that don't involve him, but it's the only way to distract him.

Let him get angry with me, at least it'll make me forget the radiating pain in my chest.

"Arguing about what?"

Inhaling sharply through my nose, I'm not keen on supplying all the information to my father, but that menacing gaze has me continuing to explain.

"Ashton and Nova have been ... hooking up."

Dante folds his arms across his chest and leans back against the desk. He still towers above me. I expect to see a flash of anger, disappointment, but instead, there's nothing. No emotion whatsoever.

"That's not exactly news. They've been sneaking around since before your wedding."

"Did everyone know but me?" I can't believe my father was aware before I was about Nova and Ashton.

He doesn't answer my question. "You and Ashton were fighting. Why?"

"He lied to me." How does he not see this as a problem? Of all people, he's a don. He should realize the importance of loyalty and honor. "It was a betrayal! I warned everyone on the team to stay away from my little sister."

Dante's eyes crinkle, and he's almost smiling. "You do realize that you and Nova aren't actually siblings?"

"We grew up together!"

Dante nods. "Yes, and Moreno is my blood cousin. Which does make her family, but that's irrelevant."

"Moreno is your cousin?" Another bombshell I'd yet to realize. Sure, they shared our last name, but that doesn't mean much. Ricci is a common Italian surname. Not once were there pictures of Moreno and Dante growing up together.

Although it's not like I've seen pictures of Dante as a child. I've also never gone looking, and that family tree assignment in grade school, a nightmare I don't want to ever think about again.

Of course, growing up under a don, where everyone acts as family, you're made to believe they are your family.

Dante nods slowly. "Did we never mention that to you?"

"You like to leave a lot out." Glaring at him, I take another swig of the scotch. "Here's one highlight of the night that shouldn't be left out. Massimo threatened my wife and son."

Dante inhales sharply and moves to step back around his desk, finding his ass planted once again in his leather chair.

"Yeah, that about sums up how I feel," I grumble.

"You know they're family. We protect our own."

His words don't reassure me. "Right, because she can be protected at Evergreen University without constant surveillance and a bodyguard."

My father raises an eyebrow, and I hold up a hand. "I will not subject my son or my wife to that type of intrusion. I'd rather her not know of the threats. There's no reason to worry her if Massimo is dead. Ashton took quite a few shots at him."

"I'll have my men follow his progress, make sure if he's still alive, we know where he is at all times."

Does he really think that's enough?

"Massimo will send his goons out if he plans on hurting my family. He's not foolish enough to do the job himself."

"You're right, son. Massimo has years of doing deeds far worse than anything I've considered doing."

I swallow the last of the scotch and slam the glass on his desk. "Is that why you insisted on sending Ashton and me tonight?"

Dante flinches. "I wanted you to see what we're up against. The kinds of men who are truly evil."

"He traffics women, and children too." I pace the small length of his office, unable to sit, still thinking about what was interrupted tonight. "He was intending to move girls through the cabin, wasn't he? I saw a door in the basement. Was it a tunnel?"

Dante rubs at his jaw and sighs. "We believe so, but none of us ventured as close as it seems you've gotten. He has been trafficking girls, children, if you will, and I thought that perhaps you witnessing it firsthand might bend you to see that our business dealings aren't all bad. We aren't the villain in every story."

I glare at my father. "No, you're sure as hell the villain. Massimo is just another, dare I say worse. It doesn't make me feel better, and knowing those girls you speak of—where are they? Because they didn't show up last night."

"He likely called off the exchange. I'm sure he has them holed up someplace else. He has other locations that he's using to make the trade, we just haven't uncovered all of them yet."

"Trade? Trade for what?" I can't seem to wrap my head around all of the details. It's like he gives me bits and pieces when he already knows the whole damn story.

"Weapons. Money. Whatever he needs, the girls are just a form of currency to him. It's the same shit your grandfather Gino was involved with until he died. The business went underground, moved away from our area for a while, but it seems they're back, doing the same insidious work they've always done."

"We have to stop them."

Dante hides the hint of a smile playing at his lips. "Yes, that's precisely what I was hoping you'd say, son."

FIVE

HARPER

Luca stretches out on the couch. He's been playing the whole sick baby routine for nearly a week, since he got back from his parents' house.

He blamed it on the weather, catching a cold.

Except he doesn't have any signs of any sickness that I've ever seen. Unless lazy is a type of sick.

But Luca has never been lazy, certainly not when it comes to hockey.

Weirder still is that he took one of Dante's cars home. Luca complained about his car having transmission issues and Dante wanting to ensure that he had reliable transportation.

Luca has kept his distance from me and, at first, I thought it was because he might have actually been sick. While I didn't hear any sniffles or sneezes, I figured he might have had a monster sore throat, and I didn't want to catch it or him to give it to Zeke.

So, I slept in Zeke's room, which just started up the entire climbing back into bed with me routine that I'd been trying to break with my son.

"What do you mean you aren't playing hockey tonight?" Liam glances from Ashton to Luca. "You can't stay home; we'll lose without you. It's the NCAA Regionals. We need you so that we can get to the Frozen Four."

"He's sick. He can't play." Ashton vouches for him, which has me wondering what the hell happened, because last week, Luca and Ashton were at each other's throats.

"Dada!" Zeke comes barreling in, running for Luca when Ashton intercepts him and spins him around before flipping him upside down.

"Again!" Zeke squeals with a fit of giggles, and I can't help but watch from the doorjamb.

I grab Liam by the arm as he wanders back toward his room. "Do you know what's going on with Luca and Ashton?"

He snorts and shakes his head. "Ask him yourself."

"I know he's not sick." I'm waiting for him to elaborate on what's happening because Luca has been strangely distant.

When Liam just stares at me, I throw my arms up in the air and storm over to the couch.

"It's been almost a week, Luca. If you're still feeling unwell, maybe it's time we take you to a doctor." I try to call his bluff.

Ashton tickles Zeke, who now wants me again. I take him into my arms while Ashton decides to play bodyguard to Luca. "He just needs more rest and maybe some of that homemade chicken noodle soup."

I glare at Ashton and glance down at Luca.

"That would be nice."

"I'll make another pot of soup after we get back from the doctor's. Whatever you have is clearly a problem, and if you won't make an appointment, then urgent care will be able to see you today."

Liam lingers in the hallway. "Harper is right. If you're that sick, coach is going to want a note for why you're not showing up to the game. He's already been asking about why you haven't been at practice all week or the gym."

Luca grumbles under his breath and sits up, wincing.

"Is it your stomach?" I ask, coming to sit beside him with Zeke.

"You shouldn't get too close," Ashton says and swoops in, grabbing Zeke from my arms as he brings him across the room. "Don't want this little guy catching that nasty bug."

"We've all been in the house together. I'm sure if it's contagious, Zeke would be the first to get it." The fact Zeke hasn't had any vomiting or diarrhea leads me to believe it's not anything contagious.

"Don't want to be too careful." Ashton is defending Luca a little too hard.

My eyes tighten as I glance from Ashton to Luca. My hand rests on his forehead. "Should I grab the thermometer? I think there's a rectal one around here somewhere that I use for Zeke."

Luca's eyes widen. "There's no need for that, Harper. I'm fine."

"Precisely. So, why aren't you playing hockey tonight? The team needs you."

"I just … I can't." He grimaces and stands. Heading to the bedroom, he shuts the door abruptly behind himself.

"Leave it alone, Harper," Ashton says, bouncing Zeke and then flipping him around as Zeke tries to do a backflip off of Ashton.

"I can't." I follow Luca into the bedroom, shutting the door, allowing us some privacy. It's the first moment we've had alone since last week.

"You shouldn't be in here," Luca says, and he climbs into bed again with the grimacing.

"You're hurting. I can see it all over your face. What's going on, Luca?"

"Nothing." He reaches for a book on the bedside table and, again, more scowling. He can't even hide it, at least not from me.

I move to the bed, bringing my legs up to sit beside him.

"I'd like to be alone." His words are rough and grumbly, but I ignore him.

"You've been alone all week. This is my bedroom too."

"Fine. Then I'll sleep in Zeke's room." He shuts the book abruptly and pushes himself off the bed.

I slide off the mattress with ease. I'm closest to the door and stand in his way. He can move me out of the way if he wants to get by. "What's going on? Is this because of that stupid secret I kept, because you've seemed to quite easily get over it with Ashton. I'm glad you're getting along, but why are you pushing me away?"

He runs a hand through his hair and tilts his head back, emitting an exhausting sigh. "I'm not mad at you. Ashton and I are fine. We're good. You and I are good. I'm just ... sick."

"Sick, how? What's wrong? Let me help." If he's truly not feeling well, I want to be there for him. "Is it depression?" I ask, concerned that maybe he's having dark thoughts and afraid to share them with me.

"No." Luca shakes his head and stares at me. "You don't have to worry about me, Harper. I'm fine."

"You're just not interested in hockey anymore?" I ask. From what I can tell, he's gone to one, maybe two classes this week. Most have an online option that he's elected to do while "sick."

I don't want to believe that he's faking it. I don't think Luca would do that; he's always had a strong ethic when it comes to studying and working, which has me frazzled.

"I love hockey. I'm disappointed that I can't play tonight, *but I can't.*" There's a longing in his voice, a sadness that tells me something is wrong. He just won't say what it is.

I'll get to the bottom of it. I have to, because I care deeply for Luca.

"And your coach won't require a doctor's note for bailing on the team? I don't want you to face any consequences for not showing up."

"I'm not bailing. I'm sick."

"So, you've said, repeatedly. Ashton claims it's stomach-related, hence the soup. Earlier in the week, you were telling me your throat was scratchy and sore." I don't remind him that I've heard him toss a few coughs in there when I'm walking by, which always make him look more miserable.

"If it's your stomach, maybe it's something that requires medicine. Like antibiotics or something? You've been nauseous for a week."

"It's nothing a doctor can do anything about."

I quirk a smile. "Are you pregnant?" I'm obviously joking, but Luca doesn't look the least bit amused by my line of questioning.

He rolls his eyes and gently guides me aside as he stalks out of the room, and Zeke comes running right for him, slamming into his knees.

"Climb, Dada!" Zeke mumbles his words together but wants Luca to lift him and topple him around like a monkey, in much the same way Ashton has been doing all week.

"Daddy doesn't feel well," I say, untangling Zeke from Luca's legs and dropping kisses to his cheeks and face before he squeals and demands to be put back down on the ground.

I consider that a win.

I put Zeke back on the ground, and he runs to Ashton, who holds his arms out with wide eyes and a huge smile, playing with my son.

Liam stands in the hallway, his back to his bedroom, arms folded across his chest. He glances from me to Ashton. "Harper, I think you should take Luca to urgent care."

"Yeah?" I nod slowly. "I agree."

"Well, I don't agree, and I'm not going." Luca storms across the hallway, past Liam as he heads into Zeke's room and slams the door shut.

"I didn't know we had two toddlers," Liam quips, and I can't help but smile.

Me either.

Ashton hands me Zeke. "Sorry, I'd love to babysit, but Liam and I need to head over to the ice arena."

"Let us know how it goes with Luca," Liam says.

I watch them head out and really wish that Nova were here to help. Maybe Luca would listen to his sister. She's at a study group this afternoon before she goes to Ashton's hockey game.

Carrying Zeke, I knock on my son's bedroom door and open it, watching Luca seated at the edge of the mattress, head bent forward, his hands clasped together.

"It's just the three of us," I say, hoping that maybe he'll feel relieved and will suddenly talk to me. Not that he chose to do that in the privacy of our bedroom.

Luca doesn't so much as glance up at me.

"Liam agrees with me that we should get you checked out at urgent care."

"Well, Liam isn't a doctor, and he doesn't get a say in what I'm doing tonight."

"Dada!" Zeke wiggles out of my hold, and I set him on the ground.

He runs up to Luca and toddles onto the mattress, climbing into Luca's arms.

"Luca." I close the distance between us, coming to sit on the mattress, my hand falling gently to Luca's back, wanting to soothe him.

The moment my fingers graze his skin, he winces.

"Does that hurt?"

"No." But his eyes tell a different story.

My fingers are featherlight as I move from his back to his stomach, and he flinches with every graze.

It doesn't appear that it's solely his stomach causing him discomfort. I lift the hem of his shirt, not sure what I'm expecting to see, but I sure as hell am not anticipating the discoloration, the marks, the imprint of knuckles as I pull my hand back.

Well, it certainly wasn't a car accident.

"What happened?" I gasp, afraid my touch is hurting him.

"You can't tell?" He laughs darkly and winces from the pain.

"Did Ashton do this?" My mind reels, trying to understand how they went from best friends to enemies and back to friends again.

They were fighting. Luca hated Ashton a week ago.

"Of course not. He hits like a girl."

I playfully smack his thigh, which I hope doesn't hide any bruises.

His nose crinkles, but he doesn't so much as flinch. "You made my point."

I lift my arm, snarling as if I'm going to hit him on his chest, and he grabs my wrist, staring at me, daring me to hurt him.

"That's such an insult, saying someone hits like a girl."

Luca falls back against the bed, forcing me to lie back with him, my wrist tethered to his hand. He pins my hand above my head.

"Try to hit me now," he growls into my ear. "I dare you."

My insides flutter with electricity as I struggle against his grasp. My free hand swings out, and while I don't intend to hit his chest, I do make it look like I will, and he grabs my free arm, rolling us so I'm fully at his mercy.

"Nice try." He *tsks* and there's a mischievous smile on his face. I haven't seen that look, that flare of heat, in days, and it warms my cheeks. "See, you and Ashton both hit like a girl." He keeps me pressed against the bed, his body just inches from mine, the heat melting off him and flowing onto me, warming every inch of me to my core.

"Do you really want to talk about your best friend when we're doing this?" I lean in, my lips brushing against his. I crave his touch, his breath, his warmth.

His mouth moves hungrily against mine in a frenzy, but his hold on my hands never loosens.

Luca climbs above me, straddling my hips, his weight sinful and making me delirious as he grinds himself into me.

"Fuck, yes." The words spill out before I realize my mistake.

We're not alone.

"Dada," Zeke's voice chimes out, and I feel his little body clamber onto the mattress, the bed dipping with his swift movements.

Zeke is about ready to join in the little party, and he moves to climb on Luca.

Luca is quick, releasing his grasp and rolling away as I yank Zeke by the waist, keeping him out of Luca's reach.

It only seems like more of a game to Zeke, squirming and laughing. "Dada!" he chants as he throws his arms and tries to escape my grasp.

This is why Ashton had been so eager and helpful with Zeke.

Luca sits up, making sure Zeke can't tackle him while I wrestle my little monster and plant his feet firmly on the floor.

It won't be long until he chases after Luca again, wanting cuddles and to climb up on him.

I run my fingers through my tangled hair, realizing that I was the last to know of Luca's injuries. "Ashton knew. What about Nova? Did Liam know too? Is that why he insisted that we take you to urgent care?"

Luca grimaces as he stands, and I carry Zeke with me, hoping that maybe some sense has been knocked into my husband and he'll listen to me to see a doctor.

He moves to the couch and plops himself back down, clearly in agony. "There's nothing anyone can do for cracked ribs."

Shit.

"Maybe we should wrap your chest, wouldn't that help offer you some support?"

"Does it matter?" Luca forces the corners of his lips to turn upward. "I can't play hockey. Not tonight. Not for the rest of the season. I'm out."

"But this didn't happen during a game." I size him up. "This happened when you were working for Dante." It's the only thing that makes sense, although I don't understand why Liam had been quite so forceful about Luca's health, unless he knew or suspected something was wrong.

Luca presses his lips together. "Right again, love." He stretches his legs out, resting his feet on the coffee table. "I'll heal, but no more hockey this season."

"I thought you'd be more upset." I'm surprised that he's taking it rather well, considering the situation.

Luca Ricci wants to play hockey professionally. His dream is to be a household name, a star player for the NHL and out of his father's clutches.

"Did you see a doctor at your father's house?" I hope that's the reason he's pushing me back with not sending him to urgent care, although I can see where having to explain the bruises might be problematic.

"I'm disappointed that I can't play the rest of the season, but it's one game. Once they lose tonight, it's over. And they're going to lose without me."

There's the ever-cocky Luca I know and really, really like.

Okay, maybe even love.

But we're not there yet.

Married.

But neither of us has said *that* word. It's not like we married out of love.

Luca married me to protect me.

"You still never answered me about whether you saw a physician at your father's home."

Luca raises an eyebrow. “I was hoping you forgot. No, I didn’t let anyone see my bruises. Ashton was there when it happened. Liam doesn’t know, but he suspected something when he and Nova came up that night.”

His words catch me off guard. “What? Liam and Nova came to your parents’ house? When?”

“Friday night. I guess you were in bed.”

I don’t remember them leaving, but I went to bed early after Zeke was asleep. The next morning, neither of them was around, but I didn’t think anything of it.

Luca smiles and laughs. “Turns out, we both saw something we didn’t want to see.”

My brow pinches, and I run my fingers along the back of his neck, knowing I can touch him at least one place that doesn’t hurt.

Okay, hopefully there are two or three places under his clothes.

His head turns toward me, a faint, lazy smile playing on his lips, relaxing into my touch. “I walked in on Ashton and Nova completely naked.”

I choke on his words, coughing. “No way. She wasn’t worried her parents would find out?”

Luca grins that boyish smile that makes my heart flutter. “She should have been worried. I could hear them going at it. I swear I thought Ashton was cheating on her, and I stormed into the bedroom and saw a lot more of the two of them than I ever wanted.”

Chuckling, I smile as Luca turns to face me, the grimace forced behind a natural smile. “Nova called Ashton to wish him a goodnight, and the reception was shit. They exchanged a few broken apart words, and she insisted Liam drive her to my parents’ house.”

“Why didn’t she wake me?” I really wish Nova was around for me to ask her, because even though I didn’t need to be there with Zeke, I am feeling a bit left out, the last one to know.

Luca reaches for my hand, holding it in his and bringing my palm to his lips, planting a chaste kiss on my bare skin. His breath is warm and sends tingles down my arm. “You had Zeke. She wasn’t going to bother you. I’m okay.”

"Are you? What happens next time, when your father orders you to do something dangerous?"

Luca tenses for a brief moment; it's fleeting, but I see it. The tautness reaches his shoulders, and I lean in, pressing a soft kiss against his skin.

"Don't worry about me." Luca forces a smile, his eyes shining, but there's something else behind that smile that makes my stomach unsettled.

"How can I not worry? You're covered in bruises, Luca." I untangle our hands and gently graze his skin, my fingers stroking along his arm, soft and gentle like the caress of a breeze. I don't want to hurt him or startle him. While we were playing rougher earlier, my intent was never to hurt him.

"These are nothing." Luca glances down at his clothed chest. "You should have seen me when I woke up on Saturday morning. I could barely move out of bed."

Inhaling sharply, my fingers wander over his leg in a soothing motion before moving toward the inside of his thigh.

Luca hangs his head, his eyes falling shut as his lips part and soft heavy breaths come pouring out. "If you keep doing that, we're going to have to hire a babysitter because I don't want my son to see the things I intend to do to my wife," he growls.

My breath catches in my throat. My fingers stall for only a fraction of a second before I resume their touch, wanting to explore him.

I want to see all of him.

Marked.

Scarred.

Bruised.

We can heal together. I can help him heal if need be. At the very least, I can make him forget the pain for a few minutes and take him somewhere else, mentally.

His fingers move to my jaw, tilting my chin to reach his lips as he captures my mouth in a kiss that makes my insides flutter. He holds me to him, commanding, rough, and exactly what I need.

Rough is good.

Rough is fun.

Rough makes you forget all of the shit happening in your life, which is what we both very much need.

But I don't want to hurt Luca.

I let him take command, accept that he's the one in control as he slides his fingers inside the waistband of my pants and his fingers do that thing that makes my toes curl.

"Luca," I rasp, my eyes momentarily closing, and then I rest a hand on his arm. "Zeke is here." We can't do this, as much as I want to, as much as I crave intimacy with Luca.

The front door swings open, and Nova stalks in, a smile on her face, and then her eyes widen when she catches a glimpse of Luca's hand between my thighs, his fingers inside my pants.

"Mind taking the kid with you to the bedroom?" Luca doesn't even remove his hand. His fingers tease my folds apart once again, with Nova in the room.

I smack Luca's arm, my grip growing tighter on his biceps as he teases me with his fingers along my pussy.

"Oh, my gosh!" Nova covers Zeke's eyes and carries him with her down the hall. "You two owe me, big time."

"Whatever you want. Name your price. It's yours!" Luca shouts as she shuts her bedroom door. "Perfect timing." His eyes shine as he captures my lips with his.

His breath is warm, his fingers tease me, touch me, caress me, as I inch closer. I want to sit on his lap, but I'm afraid of hurting him. Knowing I have to be careful and actually being careful right now are two different things. My senses are heightened, but I'm not exactly alert.

"Should we take this party to the bedroom?" I suggest.

Luca's stare floods me with warmth.

"I'd rather fuck you right here on the sofa." He tilts his head slightly, glancing me over. "God, you're so fucking beautiful with that flush spread across your cheeks."

My face is heated and now flaming with his compliment. "Thanks," I whisper and can't help but feel embarrassed. I'm not used to taking compliments.

His lips trail a path along my jaw, and he nibbles at

my ear before licking his way down my neck. "We'll have to work on that," he whispers.

"Hmm?" I don't know what he's babbling about. My only thought is of his body, touching him, fucking him, but doing everything to make sure that I'm not hurting him.

It's a lot to remember when all I want to do is ride him.

"You're absolutely sinful, your breasts." Luca is under my shirt, his fingers grazing a nipple as I arch into him and have to be careful not to touch the bruises.

My fingers itch to claw at him, but instead, I dig at the sheets on the mattress, doing my best not to cause him to scream in agony.

He slides out of his pants, his cock twitching, and he strokes it while staring at me.

He's beautiful, and he's *mine*.

I fall to my knees, my lips grazing the head, knowing that I can't hurt him if I'm sucking his cock, taking him in past my lips. There will be no pain for him, only absolute pleasure.

His fingers tangle in my hair, along my neck, as he grips me with such force that I've never felt before. "You look exquisite on your knees."

A smile spreads across my face, heat rising on my cheeks. My tongue swirls over the head, licking down his shaft, my fingers caressing him, feeling him come alive under my touch.

"Eyes on me, baby." His words are raspy, and he loses the ability to speak coherent sentences as I run my tongue over his shaft.

His fingers are all over me, his hands tugging at me, pulling me closer. There's a sense of neediness exuding from him. "That's it," he rumbles as my lips and mouth tease the head, licking the precum that drips from him.

"Fuck." His head tips back, and a low, guttural moan is absolutely sinful. "Just like that."

I love knowing that I can awaken the beast within him. Heat his very existence, make him tremble with just my tongue.

His eyes struggle to stay open as my mouth devours him. "Take it for me, I know you can." His hands are in my hair, tugging me, driving his cock deeper into my mouth. My pussy flutters at his control and power over me.

My mouth moves, his hand guiding my head, as my mouth and tongue fuck his cock. "Keep doing that." His cock twitches and I know he's close. I can feel it and sense it, watching him struggle to keep his eyes open, trained on me.

Moaning as he brings his cock to the back of my throat, he yanks my head back, and I'm entirely at his mercy.

"Harper, I'm going to..." He's right on the edge, warning me before it happens.

I say nothing, only move my lips back to his shaft, taking him in, letting him fuck my mouth as if it were my pussy, giving him exactly what he needs to find sweet ecstasy.

His hands are back in my hair, one hand using my head to fuck him, the other grazing over my back, sliding a hand under my shirt and slipping around to my breast, squeezing my nipple, making my own body quake as I mouth fuck him.

"Fuck," Luca's voice sends a shudder through my

body, and he feels the ripple, his cock pulsating as he grips me tighter, grunting and trembling.

He finally lets go, pouring himself past my lips and some of it down my throat. I wipe my face, the few drops on him I lick away.

"You did so good." Luca's hand finds my chin, lifting my head, smiling as he stares down at me. "Come sit."

He pats the empty seat on the sofa where I had been earlier, and I crawl up next to him. "Good girl." His eyes shine, and his breath against my ear sends my heart fluttering.

My lips part, a soft gasp from just his voice, his tone, the heat that unfolds within me and cascades out onto him.

Luca smiles, knowing precisely what he's doing. "Who do you belong to?" Luca's hand is back in my panties, his fingers deftly teasing my folds but not quite touching me.

I lift my hips, needing contact, craving it. "Fuck," I growl, my hands clawing at his arms, his hand, wanting him to satisfy me.

The cocky grin on Luca's face is almost too much to bear. "That's not my name, princess."

There he goes again, and I growl at him, leaning up, biting his bottom lip. I tug on it, and I can hear the sharp intake of breath before releasing his lip. "Call me princess again, you'll live to regret it."

He chuckles and presses a kiss to my lips. "Princess," Luca whispers, raising an eyebrow.

He knows he has the upper hand because I can't touch anywhere marked with bruises, and I can't see all the scars, because he still has too many clothes on, minus his pants.

This won't work.

Not for me.

My hands tug his shirt up higher, careful not to touch him. "Hands up," I command.

"Bossy." There's a smirk on his face, and he lifts his arms, letting me undress him.

I try not to stare at the bruises covering his chest. The blue or purple has turned green and yellow. There are a few with brown edges, all of them large, prominent across his chest, marked like a fist across his ribcage.

"Don't look at me like that," Luca rasps. There's pain evident in his voice, his tone, the way his shoulders sag.

"You're beautiful, and even scarred, you're mine." I rise up on my knees, kissing his lips, his shoulders, and Luca guides my legs farther apart. "I love you, Luca." The words come naturally, and he pulls back, staring at me, deep, like he can see right through me, know everything about me.

There's no hesitation on his part. He doesn't flinch at my confession. A crooked smile reaches his lips. "You're such a good fucking girl for me." His lips crash onto mine, his fingers in my hair. This kiss feels like it could last forever as I'm thrust into another world, another mere existence as I devour him along with this moment. "I think I'm falling in love with you too."

His words make my hands tremble, and I pull him tighter, hoping he doesn't see the effect he has on me. It's too much, too emotional, too raw to share that with him.

His lips devour me as he plunges one finger inside of my warmth, and I moan into his mouth.

It's a struggle to keep my eyes open, each breath heavier, and it takes far more energy as he hooks his finger inside of me, doing that gesture that brings a warmth flooding right through to my heart.

"Luca," I rasp out his name. The feeling of pure joy overcoming me, and I'm nowhere near oblivion as he guides a second finger, stretching me, making sure I'm ready for him.

My insides are warm, heated, but I'm nowhere near sated.

Only Luca has that ability—to bring me to my knees and beg for more.

He glides his fingers out, and I whimper in protest. Why did he stop?

That ever-present smile that is entirely Luca shines down on me like the warm rays of the sun on a cold, snowy day.

His fingers dance over my hips. "Pants off. I want to see that pretty pussy of yours."

He helps me with my pants, but I bend and slide them off, not making him risk hurting himself to undress me. Within a matter of seconds, I'm bare and Luca's grin has widened.

"Fuck, you should always be naked. Shirt off too. A goddess shouldn't hide her beauty."

I raise an eyebrow but don't argue. I'd rather be called a goddess than a princess. I smirk and toss off my shirt, letting it hit the floor.

"Lucky for you, you're married to this goddess." I kiss him, needing a taste, to feel his touch, to feel him.

His fingers caress my breast like a light kiss, and he teases my nipple, causing my back to arch into him. I pull away, just enough not to hurt him, but it's difficult being so close and yet not touch his chest.

Luca laughs and smiles. "I am the luckiest man." He doesn't argue or tease me. His hand moves to my jaw, his thumb guiding my mouth upward, more to his liking, as he devours me.

The pull of electricity races through my veins as we kiss. The heat turns up, flaming and uncontrollable as my hands roam along his arms, and I pause before I touch his back.

"You'll get luckier when these bruises heal."

"Feeling pretty lucky today, princess." He winks at me, and I grab his arms, pinning him against the sofa, smirking.

I don't necessarily have a plan, but I like that I've managed to catch him off-guard.

Luca is all smiles. "It's your move, princess."

I raise an eyebrow with a smirk. "Are you sure you want to keep calling me that?" I climb off the sofa, and Luca whimpers.

"Where are you going? Get back here." I sway my hips as though I were dancing, finding my way between his thighs and then over one leg.

His hands fall to my hips.

"No touching," I warn and wiggle my butt at him like a stripper would at a club. I lean away from him, my ass giving him a nice view as I give him a private lap dance.

"But touching is the fun part." Luca pouts and then runs a finger down my bottom.

"Sit on your hands."

"Aren't you bossy today?" He lifts his hips, sits on his hands, and obeys me with a smile. "Happy?"

"Getting there." I wink at him and turn around, giving him an eyeful of my breasts as my pussy grinds over his thigh.

"Fuck, you're wet." Luca tips his head back and shuts his eyes. "You're going to make me hard again."

I chuckle. "And that's a problem, why, princess?" I shoot back at him.

He glares at me and growls, leaning forward. He nips at my shoulder, leaving a mark, and I grind my pussy harder against his thigh, using him as leverage as I thrust against him.

His breath is hot on my cheek. "Are you fucking my leg?" His words come out as a growl, and the primal part of me wants to ravish him.

But I have to keep my hands from raking down his chest and back. I glance at Luca over my shoulder and flash a huge smile at him. "Fuck, yes, I am. Have a problem with it, princess?"

He growls and lifts me off his hips.

I stifle the whimper rising in my throat and let my fingers wander, teasing my pussy, spreading my lips for him to see what I'm doing to myself.

Luca rasps, his tongue darting out to the side of his lip. He's struggling with control.

His cock twitches, and he yanks my hand away from my pussy and guides my fingers past his lips, staring at me as he sucks off the juices. "You taste so fucking good."

My insides clench at his words and the fiery look in his gaze.

With ease, he lifts me over his shoulder. "Put me down!"

Of course, he doesn't listen. He must be in pain.

Grimacing, he carries me to the bedroom, putting me down on the mattress, on my back.

"You never listen."

He chuckles. "I could say the same about you."

His hands guide my legs apart. "Spread your legs for me." He gives an order and I obey.

My breath catches in my throat as he stares at my pussy, taking it all in. "You're fucking perfect for me."

He licks his fingers once more before he slides those same fingers into my pussy, watching as I squirm on the mattress. "Show me how much you like it when I fuck you with my fingers."

I let my body respond, my moans and heavy gasps of air emanating through the room. My hands move to my breasts, and Luca sees what I'm doing and grabs my arm, pushing it back against the bed.

"Only I'll touch *my wife*." There's a possessiveness in his words, and my body shudders from the revelation that I'm his and he's mine.

He presses firmly against my arm, keeping me from moving as his other hand rests tenderly at my hip. His tongue strokes my pussy, causing my hips to buck up off the mattress at the first flick of his tongue.

"Luca," I rasp, finding the world disappearing around me, and he's all that's left of it.

His tongue devours me, teases and brings me closer toward the edge. Heat floods all of my senses.

Warmth curls through me as I struggle against his hand, the one holding me down.

I let my other hand find its way into his hair, and he swiftly removes his hand from my hip and forcefully presses my wrist into the bed. He doesn't stop with his mouth, his tongue continuing the same rhythm, knowing exactly what I need.

Each breathy moan pulls me closer. My eyes close, my senses entirely overwhelmed by the man doing such carnal things to me that drive me wild. He doesn't stop, not until I'm quivering and shaking.

My pussy walls pulsate and throb. It's like my nerve endings are on fire, and my body trembles. As he lifts my hips off the mattress, he releases his grip on my wrists and steadies my hips as he continues using his tongue in that magical way that sends me reeling.

I'm floating high above the clouds. Heat licks my skin like fire, and I'm coated in sweat, gasping for air, toes curling as my insides clench down and ride the wave to shore.

It takes several seconds for me to catch my breath, as though I were drowning, the smile ever present on his face as my eyelids slowly open.

"Hey there, beautiful." Luca climbs up my frame and then positions himself to lie beside me on our bed, his head on the pillow, his eyes moving down every curve of my body.

I lean in, kissing him, tasting a mix of him and me on my tongue as I guide him onto his back, careful not to crush him.

Keeping distance between us is painful, but hurting him would be unbearable.

"No more secrets?" I run my fingers across his shoulders, careful not to touch the discoloration marking his skin.

"No more secrets."

SIX

BRISTOL

Waves of dizziness rattle over me as I squat down to file papers for my internship. I managed to get a pretty sweet deal, thanks to my mom, Emerson, who works for Eagle Tactical.

She convinced Jaxson to let me intern.

I should be grateful. It's not that I'm not, it's more the fact that I'm buried in years of pages that haven't been filed and organized, and that's my job.

It's boring as hell.

At least most of the time, I'm allowed to wear earbuds and can listen to music on my phone. I can thank Ariella, the woman who works here, for talking Jaxson into letting me do that.

I spend all morning sorting through pages and pages of stapled stacks of data, organizing it by name, alphabetically, of course.

Boring work.

But someone has to do it, and as the intern, I get the crappy job.

You should see their filing room—a complete and utter disgrace. The worst part is they have so many filing cabinets that they extend out of the filing room, into the hallway, which is where I'm squatting. My thighs are killing me, and my stomach keeps roiling.

Sweat beads at my forehead as another wave of both nausea and dizziness command me to my ass.

Ariella hurries up out of her chair, her heels clicking over the floor. I know it's her, because she's the only one in the office right now.

The guys who work here are all out running some type of job.

I'm not privy to it.

Apparently, it's above my paygrade, which I'm lucky to even be making minimum wage since I'm getting college credit too.

"Are you okay?" Ariella comes around the corner, offering me a hand.

The stacks of papers I was holding on my knee are tossed on the floor.

"Yeah, just got dizzy for a minute."

"You look a bit flushed." Ariella smiles and bends down. "Maybe you should sit for a minute."

"I'm fine." I brush off my embarrassment and get back on my feet, grabbing all the pages that scattered. At least the files are still stapled, and I don't have a bigger mess on my hands. "I've got it. Thanks, Ariella."

"If you need anything." She points at her desk to remind me where she sits.

"I know. I appreciate that. Thank you."

Smiling, she stands and retreats to her desk.

I run a hand through my hair and wipe the beads of sweat from my forehead. It didn't feel overly warm when I came in this morning, but the longer I'm on my feet, the hotter I've been getting lately.

Weird.

Maybe it's something I ate?

I ignore the strangeness and get back to the files. Opening the drawer, I sift through the last names—Russell, Russe, Russo. I'm supposed to be filing a Johnathan Russell, which is a ten-page background check. I pause at the name Russo, Ashleigh.

That's my bio mom's name.

Emerson is my mom, for all intents and purposes, but I didn't even meet her until I was six. She raised me. She's "Mom."

But Ashleigh, Dad never speaks about her.

I glance over my shoulder, making sure that Ariella isn't anywhere around, and I grab the folder, tucking it under the pages I still have to file.

When I have a little more privacy in the filing room, which offers a closed door where almost no one ever enters, I collapse on the floor, a filing cabinet at my back, and I retrieve the folder regarding my biological mother.

I open the contents, glancing them over, curious who requested and ran the report.

Request Made By: Emerson Ryan

That's my mom who works for Eagle Tactical. She's worked for them as long as I can remember. A few months ago, she transferred to Breckenridge to work out of their field office instead of the New York location. Emerson is more of a field agent, running surveillance ops. I've also seen her on the news as a bodyguard detail for one of Dad's clients in New York, the girlfriend of one of his hockey players. She wasn't being interviewed or anything, there was just a quick glance of her in the audience next to one of the hockey girlfriends in the stands.

No one else would have noticed, but I have the uncanny ability to overhear my parents' discussions.

Okay, I like to eavesdrop. Sue me.

I glance over the file. It doesn't offer too many details that I care about. It lists everything from her rental property, where she lived, the cars she owned. It's pages of complete and utter crap to me.

I keep scanning, looking for something juicy.

It's not like I've been dying to meet Ashleigh.

The whole not wanting to be in my life part is a downer. I wasn't adopted. I have an amazing father and a fantastic mother, Emerson.

I just, I don't know why Ashleigh bailed.

Dad never explained.

Actually, once, he told me that she was nothing more than a surrogate. That he wanted a baby so badly, he had a woman offer to help him.

But the fact he cut ties with her and never even gave me a picture—it's weird. And the way he always would change the subject when I brought her up, suspicious.

There is a photo of Ashleigh on page seven of the report, and I inhale sharply.

She has my blue eyes. Her hair is darker than mine, almost black, which is a stunning contrast to her eyes. I'd almost think she's wearing colored contacts if I didn't have the same eye color.

We share the same jaw structure, her face eerily similar, and I exhale heavily.

My hands tremble as I turn the page, trying to see what else there is to know.

Reason for request: Family history, Antonio Moretti correlation.

What the hell?

Antonio Moretti, as in *the* Antonio Moretti who is Liam's father?

Liam, the guy who drives me absolutely bonkers and whom I kissed a few weeks ago when he accidentally found his way to my dorm room.

My stomach falls out of my stomach as I slam the file closed.

Are we related?

I drop the file like it's on fire and hang my head, nausea sweeping over me.

"No." This cannot be happening.

I've been catching feelings for Liam.

I knew it was trouble.

Those damn tarot cards warned me to stay away from *him*.

It's not like I have his phone number or his address. Although, I'm well aware that he attends Evergreen University and I'm at Great Falls College.

Which means no accidentally running into him on campus.

Except for when he showed up unannounced and uninvited at my dorm room after one of his hockey games.

Coincidence?

Doubtful.

But what are the odds that he knew it was *my* room? He acted as surprised as I felt when I dragged him inside.

He was making a lot of noise, and I don't need anyone spreading rumors. It's hard enough when your father is a billionaire and is on the news far too often for his sports involvement.

Dad had to buy the Ice Dragons team because retiring wasn't an option for him.

It shouldn't matter to me.

He made it clear to the news and the media that I was off-limits.

I've always been off-limits to them, and they've mostly kept me out of the papers. He's done a good job of shielding me from the paparazzi.

Turns out, no one really cares about the famous hockey player's teenage daughter.

Unlike movie stars, I can live a quiet life.

Mostly.

Until Liam Moretti dropped in, and the next thing I knew, I was kissing him.

Luckily, I quickly regained my senses and shoved him out of my room and ignored his pleas to talk with me. Also, blasting music helped drown him out.

I've desperately tried *not* thinking about Liam lately, which hasn't gone well. A few times, I've opened a tab on the computer and contemplated trying to run a background check on him, but that could get me fired if anyone were to see.

Besides, I don't exactly have clearance around here, and you need a passcode to access that system.

Which leads me back to the file scattered on the floor that practically burned me when reading.

There's a connection between Ashleigh and Antonio?

Trembling, I reach for the file.

I have to know.

Because that would put the nail in the coffin with Liam. If we're related, absolutely nothing could ever happen.

I open the file, this time skimming bits about Ashleigh until I find information on her relatives and family members.

Siblings: Antonio Moretti

No.

It can't be.

My breath catches in my throat, the room spins. Thankfully, I'm already on my ass, my back against the cabinets as I slam my eyes shut.

Tears threaten to surface.

Why am I this upset over something so trivial?

Because I clearly like him.

The fact that I've been thinking about him non-stop proves that to me, but I keep wanting to deny it.

Well, it doesn't matter.

If Liam and I are related, then obviously nothing can ever happen.

I toss the file across the room, the staple tearing and the pages scattering haphazardly.

"Fuck!"

SEVEN

HARPER

"Mama." Zeke is practically climbing out of my arms like a jungle gym as I wrestle him into the car seat.

I'm not used to borrowing Luca's car, and I'm even more unfamiliar with Dante's car that he loaned Luca.

"Are you sure I can drive this? Your dad's not going to report it stolen?" I'm only half-joking. Dante still scares me.

Luca quirks a grin as he's behind me. "I promise Dad said I could keep it. One of the perks of the job and you being my wife." He leans in and kisses me, wrapping his arms around my waist from behind. "Gives me perks too."

I snort and playfully push him away, just as Zeke climbs out of his car seat.

I toss my head back, staring up at the sky, grumbling. My son is pushing my level of frustration.

Luca's hands are back on my hips, his breath on my neck. If he's trying to calm me down, it's not working. "You're not helping. Neither of you boys are helping." I'm feeling beyond a tad bit annoyed with Zeke going through the terrible twos, which is extending for longer than I'd like.

"Mama, no car."

"Can I try?" Luca's voice is soft and gentle. It's his calmness that, for some reason, irks me today.

"Be my guest." I walk away, needing to cool down, while he manages to talk to Zeke and get him to sit in his car seat. The next thing I know, he's buckling the kid up without protest.

What. The. Fuck.

Luca has become the toddler whisperer.

After he gets Zeke buckled, he drops a kiss to his forehead and pulls back, that cocky grin only irritating me further. “You’re welcome.” He’s all smiles, glowing practically.

I press my lips together to keep from making a smart-ass remark, and Luca leans in, stealing a kiss. His hands snake around my waist as he kisses me.

I’m careful, my fingers gentle against his chest because I know the bruises are healed, but I still worry about his cracked ribs.

“Are you sure you don’t want me to take him to the park?” Luca asks. “You could take a nice hot bubble bath, relax.”

My eyes tighten. I can’t stop myself from arguing with him. My hands ball into fists, irritated. “Are you telling me I need to relax?”

He smiles, his hands up in the air. “I’m saying I’m here to help. I’d never tell you that you need to relax or calm down. But you seem a bit ... stressed.”

Luca leans in and kisses my lips, the tension inside melting away the longer his lips are on mine.

His hand snakes to my lower back, and he pulls me tighter, sliding his leg between mine and backing me against the car door. He pushes a strand of hair behind my ear, his mouth caressing the lobe. "You need a good fucking, don't you, princess?"

The anger, frustration, all of it seeps out at the first part of his sentence, his words my undoing, until I hear him call me *princess* and sends it all flooding back.

Annoyance rains down on me. My top lip snarls, and he pulls back, chuckling.

"Worried I'll bite you?" I pretend to lean in and snap my jaws at him.

Luca grins. "Only if your lips are wrapped around my cock."

My breath catches in my throat. Just hearing him talk like that sends butterflies through my stomach and makes my skin warm.

I lean in, playfully tugging his bottom lip between my teeth, and hear him growl.

"Mama, what's cock?" Zeke repeats, and I grimace.

There goes my mood again.

"Sorry," Luca whispers and kisses my nose. He has the ability to bring the sunshine right back. I can't stay mad at him. Not even playful mad.

"No, you're not." I kiss him one last time. "Okay, I need to go, or by the time I leave, it'll be dusk."

Zeke plays at the park for an hour before the wind kicks up and the air temperature drops a few degrees.

"Come on, Zeke. Time to go!" I shout for him, watching as he keeps running around the playground, chasing another little boy about his age through the sandbox.

From across the park, there's a man in a long black coat and sunglasses watching us.

Or maybe he's just waiting for the bus. Except he's on the wrong side of the street for the bus stop.

He could be watching anyone or just standing awkwardly for the past few minutes, but it sends a tingle down my spine, a chill.

And the sunglasses with it growing dark feels off.

I hurry to swoop Zeke up, and we head across the street in the opposite direction, for the grocery store.

I grab a grocery cart, let Zeke sit in it while I push him, and collect the couple of items we need for dinner.

As I'm wandering down the cereal aisle, wanting to grab Zeke's favorite for breakfast, the man stops at the end of the aisle and stares at me.

He's not anyone I recognize.

Is it one of Dante's men, sent to spy on me?

Send me a warning?

He's sure as hell intimidating.

Is this some type of revenge because I ran off on our wedding day? That was months ago; Luca and I have been fine ever since. We've grown closer.

We haven't visited his family as much, we've shared a couple of dinners, but with Luca's injuries, he's been home recovering on weekends, which is fine with me.

I opt to ditch the groceries and grab Zeke out of the

grocery cart, exiting the store without buying anything.

Zeke doesn't seem to know what's going on. I keep my car keys in one hand and Zeke against my hip. I glance over my shoulder, and there's no one around.

Okay, good.

As I approach the car, I open the back door, and Zeke wiggles in my arms. "Car seat time, buddy." I smile and try to put on the happy, chipper face that Luca had, which seemed to work for him.

Zeke climbs into the car but then wiggles around. The kid won't hold still for me.

"Zeke, I need you to sit in your car seat."

"Don't want to!" he protests.

I lean into the car, trying to strap him in with the seatbelt on his car seat, but he wiggles and dances his butt, pushing off, refusing to listen.

A shadow dances over the car, and I feel the stranger's presence behind me. The fine hairs on my arm stand on end, and I involuntarily shiver.

His breath is on my neck, leaning in, trapping me between my car and the white van that parked next to us sometime after we stopped at the park.

"You really should buckle your son in, to be safe."

I pull back slightly, his sunglasses reflecting my expression right back at me.

"Anyone ever told you to mind your own business?" I growl and forcefully stomp on his foot. "Back the fuck up."

He smells of gasoline and something else oddly sour and acrid.

There's not much space between the lanes, thanks to whoever parked next to me. He backs up against the white van, and the door slides open.

He's not alone.

For a flash of a second, I can see myself or my son getting kidnapped, and I jump into my car with Zeke, slamming the door shut and locking all the doors with the key fob.

The strange man with the sunglasses smiles and laughs. He's got two gold caps on his front teeth. He lifts his sunglasses and winks at me.

Fucking bastard.

“Mama?” Zeke’s voice catches in his throat.

He can sense my fear and likely my frustration.

“Everything’s going to be fine.” I’m trying to convince Zeke that we’re safe, but I’m trembling inside.

The man outside the car is laughing, and I dig out my purse on the floor and call Luca, collapsing onto the seat next to Zeke.

“Hey, Harper,” Luca’s voice echoes through the speakerphone.

My breath cracks as I try to take a few deep breaths to steady my racing heart. “I’m ... scared.” I try to be brave, for Zeke. I don’t want him to see me breakdown. It’ll only upset him.

“I’m coming. Are you still at the park?” Concern is evident in Luca’s tone. There’s commotion through the phone, and I imagine he’s getting ready to leave the house.

“I’m in the parking lot at the grocery store, and this guy, he threatened—”

"Stay on the phone with me." Luca's voice is the only thing that calms me.

The asshole that harassed me climbs into the front seat of the van and gives me one last creepy smile and a salute before he pulls out of the space next to us, leaving me trembling.

"It's okay," I whisper, trying to regain my composure. I force a smile at Zeke, whose eyes are tearing up. "The guy who threatened us just pulled away."

There's more noise in the background of Luca's phone, and I can hear Ashton and Liam but can't make out what's being said.

"Fuck. Tell me exactly where you are, Harper."

"In the backseat with Zeke. The car doors are locked. We're parked at the grocery store, in the last aisle, across from the playground."

"I'm coming with Liam and Ashton. We'll be there in a few minutes. Just keep talking to me. Tell me everything."

I can hear commotion on their end, and within a minute or two, the engine of the car, Liam's car more specifically, is impossible to ignore through the phone.

I recant what happened with the stranger, and I swear I can hear steam emanating from Luca.

"We'll be there soon," Luca says. "Just keep the car doors locked." Luca's voice is filled with resolve. He's the strength I need right now, more than anything.

Liam's muffler is broken, but it's the sound of relief when I can hear it approaching from down the road.

When Liam's car pulls up, Luca jumps out, walks around the vehicle, convincing himself everything is okay before he tells me to unlock the door for him and we hang up the phone.

Ashton heads into the store, while Liam parks in the abandoned space next to our car.

"Ashton and Liam are going to talk to the manager and have them pull surveillance footage. I'm going to take you home."

Silently, I nod, holding back the tears, not wanting Zeke to see me break down.

My bottom lip trembles, and Luca watches me from

the rearview mirror as I sniffle. “Do you want to climb up front with me?”

Wordlessly, I climb over the console, falling into the leather passenger seat. He reaches across, his hand finding mine, intertwining our fingers together.

“Next time, call me as soon as you suspect anything. Ever. Okay?”

“I just, I thought it was my imagination. You know how your father is. I thought he might be one of Dante’s men, but that white van, the threats,” my hands tremble and I inhale sharply, my voice quivering, “it felt different.”

Luca glances at me, gives my hand a squeeze but doesn’t say anything.

“You think it’s your father?” I ask. His silence has me concerned.

“No. I think there are men out there worse than Dante.”

I find that hard to believe, but I don’t think insulting his father is going to do any good right now.

“We’ll know soon enough,” Luca says, squeezing my

hand again. "Liam and Ashton will get the surveillance tapes."

"And if the store doesn't give it to them?" I can't imagine they'll just hand it over to two college-aged kids.

"Everything will be fine."

He's far calmer than I feel right now. I watch as he drives us the couple of miles back to campus. I'm relieved when we pull up out front of the house. I climb out of the car, help get Zeke unbuckled and carry him to the door.

Luca seems a bit more on his toes, glancing around thoroughly outside the property.

"I'm sure no one followed us home." I force a smile, but his worry is starting to rub off on me. And maybe it should. What happened at the park and grocery store was creepy as hell.

Does he know something that I don't?

"The white van that pulled up alongside of me, it drove off." I gesture to the quiet neighborhood, feeling safe. "No creepy white vans."

"We're safe now, Luca. Right?"

EIGHT

BRISTOL

After throwing the file across the room, nausea sweeps over me.

I'm flooded with anger, embarrassment, humiliation.

I was starting to catch feelings for Liam Moretti, which I knew was a mistake. He's an asshole with a cocky smile, and I'd bet my life on it, he has a micro-penis.

Yep, that's what I keep telling myself, to remind me that I hate him and should never catch feelings for that jerkwad.

The problem is that kiss has been impossible to get out of my head.

Had it never happened, I'd never thought twice about him. He's usually the farthest thing from my mind. Easy when we don't go to the same school and the chance of running into him is almost zilch.

I mean, his sister attends Great Falls, but it's not like we're best friends. That ship sailed when she fucked me over freshman year in high school.

I tend to hold grudges.

The wooden door swings open, and Ariella glances at me, her brow pinched. "Everything all right in here? I heard you scream."

I wipe the stray tear that I didn't realize started to fall.

"Everything is fine."

I lie.

But I don't feel okay.

My bottom lip trembles, and her brow pinches as she bends down to gather the file, perhaps recognizing the name.

"Sometimes we see things we might not want to with this job." Ariella's voice is calm, and her tone comforting. She offers me a hand, and I take it, standing.

"Ashleigh was my birth mom." The words spill out before I realize what I've said and wince.

Ariella nods slowly. "It's a small town. People trust us with their secrets. You're going to see a lot of things that need to be kept private. Do you understand?"

"Of course." I nod vigorously. "I won't say anything."

As she shuffles the file together, she pauses and glances at me. "Emerson should talk with you about Ashleigh. She's the one who requested this file."

My stomach bottoms out. "You're going to tell my mom about this?"

My head swims, and I shut my eyes, my heart palpitating in my chest. I feel like I'm on the edge of a panic attack.

Ariella rests a hand on my shoulder. "Do you want me to give you a few minutes? I can grab you a glass of water, or there's some orange juice in the office fridge if you prefer?"

"Orange juice sounds really good."

Anything to make Ariella take longer.

"Just stay put, okay?" She takes the file with her and heads out of the filing room.

I force a smile. "Of course."

So much for reading the rest of that dossier on Ashleigh Russo. I was hoping I might have even been able to make a copy of her picture.

It's nearly lunch, and I've spent most of the morning filing, although Ariella insisted that I take a break, drink the entire orange juice, and sit at my desk and do more sorting.

While I appreciated her input, I ignored her suggestion, at least the bit about sitting at my desk.

I needed to get the filing done. I'd already sorted yesterday afternoon. I filed in the morning. That was my routine.

The front door swings open; there's chatter in the front entrance. I can't make out what's being said, and I reach behind myself, shutting the file room door.

I prefer peace and quiet to eavesdropping around here.

I could use my earbuds, but I'm not in a very listening to music mood.

Right now, I'm enjoying the sanctity of silence.

I glance at my watch. In a bit, I'll leave for lunch. I don't have a specifically scheduled hour, it's more like when I have time and can break, do it.

I want to get all the filing done, then have lunch, so I can sort after.

I'm all about routines.

While this job is boring as sin, at least it's predictable.

There's a knock behind me on the filing room door, and I glance over my shoulder as it opens. "Hey, Bristol." Emerson smiles at me, but there's something else I sense.

Ariella told her I was snooping.

"Let's grab lunch together."

"Can you give me ten minutes? I'm almost done."

Mom nods. "Of course. I'll be out here. Come find me when you're ready."

Twenty-five minutes later, I'm finally done, and I wander out of the filing room. Ariella and Em are chatting briskly until I stalk over. "Don't stop on my account." As long as they're not talking about me, I'm happy.

"We'll be back in a bit," Emerson says to Ariella. Mom leads me outside, and I'm waiting to get scolded.

Just because she's not technically my biological mother, the woman still can give a tongue-lashing as good as my dad.

She unlocks the Subaru, and I climb into the passenger seat.

"Where do you want to go for lunch?" she asks.

"Lumberjack Shack?" I love their food, and the fact Mom is buying makes it extra special.

As it turns out, just because your father is a billionaire doesn't mean you're rolling in dough. Dad made it clear that his money is his. Well, his and Mom's. I have to earn my own way.

That's not to say that he doesn't pay for my tuition, housing, and all the required school stuff, but he's not giving me an allowance if I want to buy stuff. That was cut off at eighteen, and my allowance wasn't more than a few dollars a week for doing chores.

He wanted me to live a normal life.

Sucks for me.

It's why I took the internship while going to school. It's part-time, a few hours a week until the end of summer. The pay is absolute shit, and the commute by bus sucks, but I'm not working someplace greasy, flipping burgers.

"How are you liking your new job?" Mom asks.

I glance at her as she focuses on the road. "It's good. I mean, filing is boring, but at least I know I'll be employed forever, at the rate you guys keep leaving stacks of papers on the counter and my desk to get filed."

Mom laughs. "As you get older, there are other, more enjoyable aspects of the job. But you're still young. You have plenty of time for that."

I'm not quite sure what she means. "And there's always time for filing, right?"

"On to a more serious note, we should talk about what you saw this morning. The file on your biological mother." Em's tone is serious, and I roll my lips together, waiting for her to scold me or yell at me for snooping.

"I want you to know the reason I had the background check run."

I shift in my seat, surprised she's not screaming at me.

Her tone is much more reserved, calm, composed. Like she's already practiced this conversation a thousand times in her head.

"It said something about Antonio Moretti."

Mom nods. "Yes. Do you remember when we first met?" She pulls off the main drag, up the mountain pass, and to the log cabin restaurant. The place had some renovations and has grown over the years, but their food is still dynamite.

Parking the car, we both step out and head inside.

We grab a booth and are given menus. It's not like I need mine, I know exactly what I'm going to order.

Their Brunswick stew is to die for.

Plus, I absolutely love the chips they give me to dip in their stew. It's the best part.

After we give the waitress our drink and food order, Mom is staring at me, concern etched on her brow. "Do you remember when we first met, Bristol?" she asks me again.

"I was six," I say, trying to think back to the time that I first laid eyes on her. "Not really. I remember that you were my nanny for a short time before you started dating my dad, then you guys hired Lia to look after me."

A wry smile crosses Mom's face. "We didn't want to tell you, but your father hired me as your bodyguard."

A huge grin covers my face. "No way." I mean, I know she's done that kind of work for other people, but she was *my* bodyguard?

I'm staring at her, my jaw practically on the floor. "How did I not know?"

"Your dad didn't want me to tell you. Actually, you came running into the room asking if I was your nanny, and your dad went along with it."

"So, you guys lied to me?" I raise an eyebrow, tilting my head at Mom. "And why the hell would a six-year-old need a bodyguard? Was the boogeyman chasing me?"

The smile on Mom's lips slowly begins to vanish. "Your father had concerns about the Italian mafia coming after you."

"Right. Come on, what was the real reason, Em?"

I know she doesn't like when I call her that, but I've made it clear I'm not calling her Mom at work. And this feels like a very work-esque conversation.

She ignores my use of her name, not the least bit bothered by it. I usually call her Mom, but for the longest time, she was Em to me and M&M to my dad. He still gives her that nickname, which makes me want to puke. The flirting with those two never ceases to end. Gross!

"Your biological mother, Ashleigh, had a sibling who was kidnapped before Ashleigh was born. They never found him."

My eyes widen. “No way. Not even Eagle Tactical could find him?”

“Eagle Tactical wasn’t around when he was taken, sweetheart.”

Right. Silly me. “Okay, so Antonio Moretti is my ... uncle?” I guess, having already put the pieces together. I’m super grossed out by the news, mostly because it puts an instant end to any thought of Liam and me together.

Bummer.

“Yes, and no. Ashleigh had run one of those ancestry DNA tests. She wanted to find out if her brother was still alive. The results came back that she had a family member named Antonio Moretti.”

“Where’s the yes and no part? That sounds like a solid yes to me.” I fold my arms across my chest. “My Uncle Antonio is what, that Italian mafia?” I’m joking, only because she mentioned the mafia earlier, but he’s not mafia.

I mean, does the mafia even still exist today?

“Antonio Moretti is involved in organized crime,” Mom says, with a straight face, “but there is more than one Antonio Moretti in New York City. The background check let me narrow it down by date of birth, not just year. Which means there are twenty men named Antonio Moretti in New York City, not to mention New Jersey and other states where your biological uncle may have been relocated as a child or moved to as an adult."

I stare at Mom blankly.

What the hell is she getting at?

"Your uncle isn't involved in the Italian mafia. He was kidnapped as a child, rehomed, and currently lives in Connecticut."

I'm staring at her, dumbfounded.

"I'm not related to the Antonio Moretti whose son I went to school with?"

Mom smiles. "You remember Liam and Sophia's dad? We invited them over for dinner once, interesting night."

That had been the only time I recall meeting his father. His mom had brought Sophia over to the ice rink for us to go skating after that, the two of us becoming fairly close.

I don't remember much from that night. I was young and hated Liam. I punched him in first grade after he harassed me tirelessly. The teacher wouldn't put an end to it, so I did.

"So, I'm not related to that pompous asshole?"

Mom's gaze tightens. "Language, Bristol. But no, you are not related to any of them. Does that make you feel better?" she asks, perhaps sensing my discomfort. Of course, she doesn't know why.

"Yes."

Our food gets brought to the table, and I hungrily enjoy the chips, dipping that into the stew.

"So, do you promise no more snooping at the office?"

"I wasn't snooping!"

Okay, maybe I was, but it was, after all, my bio mom's file. What was I supposed to do, ignore it? Fat chance in hell.

Work is boring as hell, but Mom isn't in the office the rest of the afternoon.

I jam the copier, making sure to really screw it up. Just as it goes to copy, I force-feed it several extra sheets, and it makes a ton of obnoxious sounds, like it's being eaten alive by wolves.

"Ariella!" I grumble and hope my trick works.

"Oh, shit. Not again." She jumps up from her desk, her heels clicking.

"I need to use the washroom. Can you try to fix this monstrosity?" I brush past her, toward the washroom and then sneak through a hallway, back to her desk.

Jackpot!

She *finally* left her computer unlocked.

Don't ask how many times in the past several weeks I've tried this trick.

It always works, but the unlocking of her desktop, I haven't been as lucky.

I quickly open up the page for our background checks and type in *Liam Moretti*.

I'm not looking for any prior arrests. I don't think he has any, at least I hope not. What I do want is his contact information.

I get an address and scribble it down on a scrap piece of paper, shove it in my pocket, before closing the window on her computer and hurrying back.

"Got it!" Ariella yanks the pages free, her hands grimy from the ink. "This old thing. I keep telling Jaxson he needs to bring someone in to look at it. Funny how it only acts up for you."

I laugh. "Yeah, craziest thing."

NINE

LIAM

Ever since that weird encounter with Harper at the grocery store, things have felt a bit ... off. Actually, it started before that, with Luca refusing to play our last game of the season, which we lost without him.

I'm still a bit sore about the whole ordeal.

I know he claimed to be sick, and I feel for him, but it was like Ashton was playing Luca's personal bodyguard, defending him and wasn't the least bit worried about him seeing a doctor.

I hate secrets, especially when I'm the one being kept in the dark.

But I get it, Luca and Ashton work for Dante. It's no secret around here that they're both actively involved in Luca's father's business. Which has me curious if all of it is intertwined.

I drag Ashton into my bedroom. It's hard to get five minutes of his time with Nova around. "Are you going to tell me what's going on between you and Luca?"

Nova wasn't home the day we fled to the grocery store to check on Harper and grill the manager about the security footage.

After we made it clear that Harper had been stalked and harassed, the manager reviewed the tapes and then let us watch them after he was convinced we weren't making shit up.

It was no one any of us recognized.

And that was the last word Luca and Ashton had spoken of it for the past several days. At least to me.

"What are you talking about? Me and Luca?" Ashton glances at me like I'm the one who's crazy.

"Harper. The stalker from the grocery store. What the hell is going on?"

Ashton's gaze tightens, and he grimaces. "You should talk to Luca."

"Fine." I groan and throw open my bedroom door, storming out of the room.

Luca is seated on the couch with Zeke.

"A word," I bite out and nod toward my bedroom.

"I'm a bit busy—" Luca attempts to blow me off, and I hurry across the room and yank him to follow, shutting the bedroom door behind myself. "Zeke—"

"Your son will be fine for five minutes."

That's all I need.

Luca folds his arms across his chest, leans back on the closed door and raises an eyebrow. "What's going on?"

"That's what I'd like to know!" I huff, glaring at Luca and then shifting my attention to Ashton. "The two of you keep so many secrets around here. Which is fine, until you start dragging me into this mess. What was that at the grocery store with Harper? Who was that guy? Why is he threatening her?"

I have so many questions, and Ashton and Luca just stare at me. They quietly exchange a glance between themselves, followed by more silence.

Luca's tense jaw tells me if I don't keep pushing, I won't get any answers. His gaze locks with mine, and he doesn't waver.

Ashton glances away, studying the music posters on my wall, pretending to be interested in anything other than this conversation.

"Silence won't cut it. Not with me. You owe me an explanation. I dropped everything to drive you both to help Harper, and I'd do it all over again, but you can't tell me it was nothing. I saw the security footage." I stare Luca down, waiting for him to flinch or cave and reveal something to me.

More silence and I step closer, invading his personal space. "You owe me answers."

"I don't owe you anything," he bites back.

"Really? Next time your wife is in trouble, should I just leave you to figure it out on your own?" I had dropped everything I was doing, jumped in my car with Ashton and Luca, and hauled ass across town to make sure that Harper and Zeke were all right.

Luca sighs and tips his head back against the door, glancing up, avoiding my stare.

He knows I'm right.

"Harper and Zeke were threatened a few weeks ago by another mafia boss, Massimo DeLuca. It's a long story, but the short version is Harper doesn't know about the threats."

Exhaling, I step backward, giving Luca space as I move to sit at the edge of my mattress. I shouldn't be surprised by the news, it's not like I'm unaware that Dante is mafia, but I don't like hearing my friend and her son are being threatened by another mafia boss.

"And what about you? Is that why you couldn't play our last game this season? Did he threaten you too?" I knew Luca wasn't sick. I just wasn't sure what the hell happened that made him give up his favorite sport.

"He did a little more than threaten me." Luca points at his chest. "A couple of cracked ribs in addition to some nasty bruises."

I grimace. The cracked ribs were probably why he couldn't play hockey. I've seen him with bruises after a game. It's never kept him from working out or attending our next practice.

When he's finished telling me about Massimo DeLuca, his uncle and the man who he believes is behind the threats, I realize my lip is bleeding.

I've been biting down without even realizing it. I wipe away the blood and wince, but not from the pain.

It turns out the threats to Harper and Zeke aren't just words.

"You can't tell Harper." The heat in Luca's gaze is unnerving. Luca steps toward me, towering above the mattress.

He expects me to keep this just between the three of us?

My head swims.

Shouldn't Harper be aware so she could be more careful? "Why the hell not? She deserves to know if she's in danger."

"I don't want to worry her." Luca scowls at me. "And it's not your place to tell her."

Ashton glances away, his attention moving from the poster to my record player against the wall on a wooden stand. He's clearly trying to distract himself to keep out of the conversation as much as possible.

It seems he's in agreement with Luca, based on his silence.

"That's a hell of a secret that you're asking me to keep." I hang my head for a solid minute, debating what the right thing to do is for everyone involved. I finally glance up at him. "Fuck, Luca. It's shit like that; it's going to make Harper hate you."

Just when they are finally getting settled into married life—happy, blissful—he's going to fuck it all up.

At least I'm trying to help him from wrecking his marriage.

"Swear to me that you won't tell Harper." Luca stands over me, and I roll my eyes, annoyed that he doesn't trust me.

"I swear it."

"She doesn't need to worry about DeLuca and his

men. But I need both of your help." Luca glances from me to Ashton, waiting to see if he's onboard.

Ashton glances over his shoulder at Luca. "Whatever you need, we're family."

"There's already surveillance around the property," Luca says, "but I need to know Harper and Zeke are safe wherever they go."

"You want one of us to play bodyguard all summer?" I quip. "That seems like a role more suited for you."

Ashton laughs under his breath.

"This isn't a joking matter!" Luca's fuming, but I doubt Harper is going to be excited that she has one of us with her at all times.

Knowing Harper, she'll evade us and run off as soon as she discovers what we're up to. That girl has a sassy streak.

"Liam's right. How are we going to follow Harper around without her knowledge?" Ashton smirks, waiting for Luca to come up with some grand plan.

"We take turns watching her back; it won't be hard if it's here, at the house. Someone needs to be with her and Zeke at all times." Luca glances at both of us, and we nod in agreement. "I need this from you both. Don't make me beg."

"Only because I like Harper and Zeke. Otherwise, I'd make you get on your hands and knees for me."

Ashton chuckles under his breath. "I'll watch you beg, Luca."

Luca's hands ball into fists, and his nostrils flare.

I've seen his rage on the ice, and I don't want to be on the other side of him throwing a punch.

"Relax, we're just messing with you." Ashton smacks Luca on the back. "We'll make sure your family is safe."

Luca exhales loudly. There's no smile. No mirth. Just concern for his loved ones.

"And what about when she wants to take Zeke to the park or go for a walk? Are we supposed to follow her?" I ask. I don't feel like he's really thought his plan through very well. It'll seem odd if we're always escorting her. Harper will take notice, eventually.

Ashton snorts. "I don't think stalking Harper is going to help the situation."

Luca grumbles, clearly annoyed with both of us. "I'll offer whenever I'm home, but it would be nice if you accompanied her, but *don't* follow her." His gaze is like two sharp daggers.

"Relax, I'm not your wife's stalker. I was joking about the following. Sort of." I force a smile as I hold Luca's stare. "We'll look after Harper and Zeke. You don't have to worry."

Ashton's brow pinches as he strides across the room. He peruses my vinyl collection, clearly helping himself to see what I have. "I can probably convince Nova to help a bit too, if you're comfortable with me confiding in her about what's going on?"

"Absolutely not!" Luca paces the length of my bedroom. "Anything you say to Nova, expect her to tell Harper."

"Nova can keep a secret." Ashton defends his girlfriend, and I watch with rapt fascination.

Nova kept her relationship hidden from Luca for months, but Harper knew and kept it quiet too. There have been a lot of secrets under this roof.

"Just no." Luca heads for the door, noting that the discussion is closed.

I'm glad for the summer break, the heat, the fact that I don't have to go to class.

Bodyguarding for Harper and Zeke doesn't seem that bad, except there wasn't any mention of pay. Maybe I should have negotiated with Luca or asked to be put on his father's payroll, like Ashton.

With Luca still recovering from his injuries, Ashton and Luca get weekends off from working for Dante. I'm grateful, or else I'd be spending all of my weekend with bodyguard duties.

Not that my weekends are jam-packed as of late.

Ashton and Nova spend just about all their free time hooking up or cuddling together. I try not to feel jealous—not that I like Nova as anything other than a friend.

I just miss what I had with Iris, which wasn't much. A friend-with-benefits arrangement, which was great during our holiday breaks and summer, when we had lots of free time and could hook up.

I've been needing to scratch that itch, and late at

night, my thoughts have been entirely on Bristol Greyson.

I know, I should not be fantasizing about the girl who would murder me in my sleep if given the opportunity.

That's all it ever is, though, a fantasy, because I can't reach out to her. She's *trouble*. Plus, she hates me.

The girl punched me in the first grade!

No, I still haven't forgiven her for it.

I mean, she completely humiliated me. The least she could have done now is stroke my ego a bit, make up for it. But she never would.

That girl is the devil.

And that kiss that we shared, I *need* to get it out of my head.

But I can't.

I've tried kissing a few puck bunnies, but it's never gone past that, because every time their lips are on mine, I think about *her*.

My bedroom door jets open, and Zeke comes

running in, climbing on my bed. He starts jumping and squealing as he throws his arms in the air.

For fuck's sake, where are Luca and Harper?

I lift the kid, holding him out like a sack of flour. "Luca!" I growl, carrying the toddler, who kicks and wiggles in constant protest.

"Down. Put down." Zeke has gotten so big over the past couple months. "Fuck down." And his vocabulary has become much more colorful, thanks to some of us living under this roof.

"I don't think you're supposed to use that word," I scold Zeke.

He sticks his tongue out at me.

He's Luca's kid, no doubt. I mean, maybe not biologically, but the mannerisms that he's picking up scream Luca.

Okay, maybe they also scream a little of Ashton and me too.

We're totally corrupting him.

"Your little dude just barreled into my room,

uninvited." I hand him off to Luca, who puts him down on the ground, letting him run freely.

"Sorry, Liam. Lock your door if you don't want him barreling in." Luca grabs the television remote. "Hey, buddy, do you want to watch some cartoons?"

"You're not putting him in front of the television all day." Harper comes barreling out of the kitchen in the same manner Zeke came running into my room.

It's like a mini-me terrorizing this place.

I glance around the house. Ashton and Nova seem to have disappeared. Both of their bedroom doors are closed. They could be screwing, but I would guess they're out, avoiding the wrath of the little engine that could destroy my sanity.

I grab my shoes by the door.

"Where are you off to?" Luca asks, raising an inquisitive eyebrow. I get the feeling that he's silently asking for an invitation, a chance to run away, if even for a few hours.

But someone has to keep Harper and Zeke safe.

"Out." I smirk and offer a wave. "Have fun, you two." I wink at Luca and then hurry out the door.

Am I the asshole? Probably, but Luca married Harper. He committed to her; he may as well learn to help her with Zeke. And he has been more actively involved lately.

For a while, Ashton had been doing a bit more of the babysitting and heavy lifting with Zeke, but it seems like Luca has finally taken over more of a role with his son.

About frickin' time.

I head to the coffee shop to grab an iced mocha and briefly glance around while I wait for the barista to make my drink.

My gaze lands on the one and only, Bristol Greyson.

My heart begins to quicken its pace with every glance at her.

Hell no.

I avoid looking at her, shift my feet, turn to face the other direction, maybe she won't notice me.

Footsteps come up from behind, and I inhale sharply. It's her scent.

I can smell her a mile away—well, not really—but oh my gosh, she smells amazing, like peaches and honey.

Her scent is intoxicating, but in the best heavenly way possible. If someone bottled it, I'd douse my pillow and bedsheets with it. The dreams I have of her would be so much more vivid.

I inhale, trying not to seem desperate or obvious when I force a smile. "Greyson."

"I prefer Bristol," she says.

"Good to know, Greyson." I don't give her the satisfaction.

That's the one thing we have going for us—banter that never ceases to end. Sometimes I can't tell if it's flirtatious or just reckless. Is there even a difference when it comes to Bristol Greyson? Any flirting would be reckless.

She rolls her eyes at me. "Whatever, Moretti."

My eyes flicker at the mention of my last name. She's trying to harass me again. Well, it won't work. I'm used to my friends calling me Moretti because it's the name on my jersey.

"Liam," the barista calls.

"Well, that's my cue." I grab my drink, and Bristol is right on my heels. The girl was never like Velcro before, but now I can't seem to tear her off me.

What is this world coming to?

"You're not going to ask me what I'm doing on *your* campus?" Bristol asks.

I shake my head. "Nope."

Am I dying to know why she's here? Yes, but I refuse to give her the satisfaction. Have I been using her as my fantasy for the last several months? Abso-fucking-lutely.

Again, the bottle of Bristol Greyson perfume would be brilliant.

Someone should market it.

I size her up, drinking every inch of her in.

Damn, she looks good in that short little black leather skirt and top that barely covers her midriff.

She's all in black and dark red, a lethal combination.

Those fuck-me leather platforms aren't helping, either.

I shift uncomfortably as my cock twitches in my jeans.

Down, boy, don't get feelings for the devil.

"Well, I came here to see you." Bristol stares at me, and based solely on her expression, I can't tell if she's serious or joking.

But she has to be joking. It's Bristol. She'd sooner swim naked in boiling hot springs than intend to pay me a visit. Unless she's here to make my life hell.

That could be a possibility.

I force a smile because anything else and I'd be bending her over that table. That skirt is far too short and yet, too long because it covers her ass.

Heat flames every inch of my body.

She has to be fucking with me.

It's definitely something that girl would do to me; she's always tormented me. Although I've certainly done my fair-share to her over the years.

We hate each other.

"Have a good day, Bristol." I don't intend to use her first name, but it slips out, and, holy hell, she grabs me by the arm.

My gaze narrows. "What the hell do you think you're doing?"

She bites her bottom lip, tugging it between her teeth, and my cock strains against my jeans, wanting to be stroked.

It's been too long since I've fucked a girl, and the way Bristol is looking at me, I'm hungry with desire.

Starving.

"I wanted to talk to you." Bristol doesn't release her grip on my arm. Her touch is hot and firm, and I yank my arm free.

"Right, well, there's nothing for us to talk about." I take my coffee with me and head out of the café as fast as possible.

"Liam!" Bristol calls after me, but I'm gone.

I need to get far away from Bristol Greyson before I do the unthinkable.

I should go spend the rest of my afternoon at the gym.

It's not a great distraction, but it would help me burn off the excess energy pouring through me, just thinking about *her*.

There is no way I like her.

None.

Zero.

It's just the fact I haven't gotten laid in way too long that I find even *her* attractive.

I need to hook up with a girl, and fast.

The problem is that with the hockey season over, I'm not getting a plethora of puck bunnies throwing themselves at me.

That's not to say that I couldn't go into a bar, find a girl, and hook up.

But that's not how I operate. I prefer the friends-with-benefits scenario, but that option I axed.

And my current friends already have significant others.

Which leaves me back to either choosing a girl at a bar or going online and searching profiles.

I refuse to do online dating.

I'm not saying there's anything technically wrong with it. I'm a guy, I like looking at pretty girls, but choosing one solely over their image first and profile second, it's just gross.

I'd rather get to know a girl, talk to her, then fuck her.

Truth is, I'm more of a, get to know the girl, then have fun. It's why I opted for friends-with-benefits over screwing random girls every night, like Ashton used to.

We're not the same.

I'm glad he has finally settled down a bit with Nova. She's changed him, definitely for the better.

I sip my coffee and hear Bristol chasing after me.

"Liam, wait." I grimace and spin around to face her. "No one can't say you're not persistent. And annoying." I add that little tidbit, just to piss her off.

Seems to be working. Her nose scrunches as rage settles on her face. I hope her coffee is iced because I'm a bit worried she might throw it on me. "I don't know why I ever considered sleeping with you!" She huffs and turns on her heels.

"Excuse me?"

Bristol's eyes widen, and she tries running away, but, yeah, I'm not having that.

"Sleeping with me?" I grab her arm, yank her back toward me, catching her as she trips over her feet. I steady her, my hands wrap around her waist, staring down into those deep ocean blues.

What is she talking about?

We never once almost slept together, except in a few of my fantasies, but those are locked up in a vault inside my head.

There's no way she has access to them.

Her cheeks are bright red, and she's breathing fast, a little too fast. "I think I'm going to be sick," she mutters, and I can feel her trembling in my arms.

I keep my arms wrapped around her waist, guiding her to a bench. Her legs are like jelly as she stumbles, and I put her into a seated position on the bench, my legs trapping her from falling forward.

Her skin is glistening and pale, while, moments earlier, she looked positively radiant and flushed.

"Fuck," she rasps, gasping for breath, like she's been running a marathon.

Eventually, I bend down to her level, still blocking her from falling off the bench. I'm not sure that she's all right.

"Do I need to call someone?" I ask, unsure what's going on.

Is she having a panic attack? I'm not really sure what to do for her, how to help her. Her eyes are wide. She's awake, but she's not seeming to focus on me.

"Bristol, tell me what's going on. Other than you want to sleep with me."

"Not funny, Moretti. I don't … I-I don't know," she stammers. Her hands are visibly shaking, and her legs tremble just slightly. I wouldn't have noticed except I can feel the tremors as she leans against me.

My hands move firmly to her arms. "I think you're having a panic attack."

Bristol shakes her head. “It’s not that. I don’t know what it is, but it’s been happening more often.”

I suck in a nervous breath. “More often. You mean this has happened before?” I reach for her wrist, taking her pulse while glancing at my watch.

“What are you, some kind of a nurse?” she jokes and winces. She sounds out of breath still, but it’s gotten a little better.

“I’m going to school for medicine. I want to study to become a doctor. But I just finished my first year of undergrad.” I haven’t started any classes that would be helpful. I have years to go before I’m actually studying to be a physician.

She should know this, we’re the same age, we went to the same private schools growing up. Her father is a billionaire. My dad, he’s mafia.

“I want to take you over to the school’s urgent care.”

“Absolutely not!” Bristol shoves me away. “I’m fine.” She stands, and I wrap an arm around her waist.

She’s trembling. It’s slight, but I notice it with her in my arms.

"Are you sure you're not just nervous because you've fallen in love with me?" I joke, trying to make light of the situation.

Bristol rolls her eyes and groans. "I assure you, Liam, that will *never* happen."

I try not to take offense. I mean, it's Bristol Greyson, my mortal enemy. Not that I have an immortal one, but the two of us would kill each other, even if we were the last two people on the planet. Humanity wouldn't survive us.

"Ouch." I'm smiling, teasing her, trying to make light of the situation. "Where are you heading next?"

"Honestly—"

"No, lie to me."

She snorts. "I should head home."

"You came all this way to campus for a cup of coffee?" I glance at her, my arm firmly around her waist. "Maybe you should lay off the caffeine. How many cups did you have?"

"Just the one."

"And this morning?" I ask, trying to figure it all out.

"I've only had the one cup of coffee today." She forces a smile. The color has returned to her cheeks, and the tremulousness has eased up. If she's shaking, I don't feel it.

I doubt she could hide it from me. At least not with the way she was earlier on the bench.

"Are you sure it's okay for you to drive home?"

Bristol cracks a grin. "Are you catching feelings for me, Moretti?"

"I don't want to see you crash into another unsuspecting family," I offer in way of an explanation. "Let me drive you home."

"It's fine. I took the bus. You don't have to worry about me killing some pregnant woman behind the wheel of a car, because I don't drive. I mean, I have my license, but I don't ever drive anywhere. No car. Always had a chauffeur growing up, rich kid problems." The smile makes me think she's not entirely happy about that little fact.

"Do you mean to tell me your dad didn't buy you a car for your sixteenth birthday?" I'm surprised. I always imagined Bristol to be spoiled.

"He wouldn't even let me get my license until I turned eighteen," she grumbles. "Overprotective asshole. Don't get me wrong, I love my parents, but he just made my life hell in high school."

"If you say so." There's no sense in arguing with her. Although I don't remember her life being 'hell' while we were in high school.

While we had different social circles in high school, I mostly spent my four years avoiding her. Luckily, we didn't have many classes together.

However, middle school is a different story. We fought, constantly. Same in elementary school. There were a lot of trips to the principal's office, both of us constantly in trouble.

"I'm going to drive you back to campus."

I walk with her slowly in the direction of my house, where my car is parked. I'm not keen on her seeing where I live. Next week, she'll probably throw toilet paper over the trees just to give me grief.

"You don't need to do that." Bristol's body tenses, but I keep walking, ignoring the feel of her warm back against my fingers.

The sun is bright, causing me to squint as we walk. "I'm driving you, but you have to promise not to laugh or make fun."

"Make fun of what?" Bristol glances at me curiously.

I inhale sharply, hoping not to humiliate myself. I could ask to borrow Luca's vehicle, but then I'll have some explaining to do. Taking her back in my car will just be easier overall.

"My car."

She shrugs and walks with me back to the house. It's a good twenty minutes, but she gets steadier on her feet for most of it. The walk back is covered with trees blocking the sun, making the air feel several degrees cooler.

I take the last sip of my coffee with one hand, the other still planted on her back. I'm almost afraid to let go.

I'm not sure why, probably because she'll end up on the ground unconscious, and I don't want to have to deal with explaining that to anyone.

"Let me grab my keys real quick." I carry my house key separate from my car keys. I head inside the house, and Bristol is right behind me, following me inside.

"Daddy!" Zeke shouts and jumps off the sofa to tackle my legs.

He's getting stronger every day. "Liam," I say, correcting him. The kid knows I'm not his father. Why the hell he's torturing me today, I have no fricking idea. "Daddy is somewhere around here."

"Hi," Bristol smiles and bends down to Zeke's level. "I'm Bristol."

"Hi," Zeke says, and his cheeks grow red. He buries his face in my legs.

"Since when are you shy?" I ask, rubbing his back and lifting him into the air, flipping him upside down.

I plant him back on the sofa after another air flip and grab my keys hanging by the door. "Catch you later," I say, hurrying to leave before there's a barrage of questions for me and, more importantly, Bristol.

Harper hurries out of the bedroom, her face flushed. "Sorry, I was just folding clothes!"

Yeah, sure you were.

I've seen that look before—the messed-up hair and wrinkled shirt. She and Luca were taking their clothes off. I'm not sure there was any folding involved.

"I'm Harper." She gives a quick wave to introduce herself.

"Bristol. Hi," Bristol says, standing by the door.

Harper's eyes widen with a warm smile. "Please, come on in. Don't mind Zeke. He's just watching cartoons. You guys are welcome to the television—"

"We're just leaving," I say, grabbing the door handle.

"I don't mind staying for a little bit." Bristol's nervous smile makes my heart flutter.

No.

She should not be capable of stirring anything other than anger within me.

"You should mind," I say. "We hate each other."

Harper gives a peculiar look to me but keeps quiet. Thankfully, she knows when she's not wanted.

"It's Saturday. Unless you have plans," Bristol

brushes past me with ease and plops down on the sofa next to Zeke, making herself right at home.

What the hell, Bristol.

"I mean, I could have plans."

"Hey, there." Bristol focuses on Zeke, ignoring me.

Yeah, that's more like it. She's not here for me. She clearly likes kids.

Zeke smiles up at her, ruddy cheeks, and bats his eyelashes.

"Do you have plans?" Bristol asks nonchalantly over her shoulder. She doesn't even glance back at me. The girl slips out of her shoes and plops her feet up on the sofa.

Am I seriously going to have competition with *him*?

"Nope. Absolutely not."

"Good. Then I can stay, for a little bit."

That wasn't what I was saying no to. Oh, fuck it.

Luca steps out of the bedroom, raising an eyebrow when he sees an unfamiliar girl on the couch with

Zeke. "Sorry, I was making the bed. Didn't hear you guys come in."

I roll my eyes at Luca. "At least get your stories straight."

Harper and Luca exchange a glance and laugh. Harper's cheeks redden and she giggles, grabbing Luca's hand and tearing back into the bedroom before shutting the door.

I swear we live with them, so they have a full-time babysitter.

"They're cute together," Bristol says and then pauses and laughs. "That's your teammate, Luca Ricci."

I inhale sharply. "Yes. Why are you asking?" If she's got the hots for him, someone's about to get murdered.

"He's a really good player for the Narwhals. I mean, your team would suck without him."

I shuffle my shoes off and walk around the coffee table to grab the empty spot on the sofa, with Zeke next to me. "He's all right."

"You guys lost the last game of your season because

Luca didn't play. And not by a little bit. You got creamed."

"Don't remind me," I growl at Bristol. "How could I forget you were always this annoying?"

Bristol doesn't so much as look at me as I watch her, study the lines of her face, the faint smile tugging at the corner of her lips. She's a sight of beauty, and I can't tear my gaze away. I'm waiting for her to snap at me, make some smart-ass remark like she always does.

"Hey, cutie." She ruffles Zeke's hair, and I'm one-hundred percent jealous of him.

Bristol then glances up at me. "You shouldn't talk like that in front of the little one. They learn everything."

My jaw drops. "You're in here two minutes, telling me what to do, how to talk, that I suck at hockey. Wow. Maybe you should ride that bus back to Great Falls."

"Maybe I should." Bristol sighs and glances at her watch.

Zeke climbs onto Bristol's lap and rests his hands on her cheeks. It's the same move that I've seen Luca do with Harper.

And sure enough, Zeke leans in and plants a giant kiss on her lips.

Bristol laughs and wipes the kiss away with the back of her arm. "Okay, Zeke, I think it's time for cartoons." She spins him around and plants him back on the sofa.

I grab Zeke, pulling him into my lap. "Consent, kid. You got to respect the ladies."

"Consent," Zeke repeats, but I'm not sure that he understands what it means. "Tickle me!" Zeke squeals and wiggles on my lap.

He never runs out of energy. I tickle his hips, watching him squirm and giggle, his arms and legs flailing wildly.

"More tickles!" Zeke proclaims, never seeming to get tired of the fits of laughter.

Bristol watches quietly. "You're really good with him."

"He's one of my closest friend's kid. We all live together. Kind of have to be, or this would be hell." I gesture to the house, our living arrangement.

"Hell," Zeke repeats and giggles, his eyes lighting up with excitement. "Hell." It's a new word that he's discovered, thanks to me.

"Shit." I curse, knowing that Harper is going to yell at me for teaching the kid another bad word.

"Shit. Shit. Shit," Zeke chants, and I throw my head back, close my eyes, and groan.

When I open my eyes, Bristol is all smiles.

"Don't say that." I glare at Zeke. "Those are bad words."

Zeke giggles. "Uncle Liam in trouble." His words roll a bit together and aren't enunciated properly, but I've learned to understand him pretty well.

Bristol wrinkles her nose and holds a finger up to Zeke to show him to be quiet. "Those aren't nice words," she says. Her voice is calm; there's no hint of anger or malice. "We don't say those things because they hurt people. Do you understand?"

Zeke stares at her and nods.

I have no clue whether he just comprehended everything she said or not, but he plops back down in my lap and resumes his attention on the cartoons.

I'm sure his attention span will be broken again in less than five minutes.

"You're really good with him," I admit, surprised that she's not a monster all the time, like she was with me growing up.

"I can say the same about you." Bristol glances me over, and I see an unfamiliar smile, almost like she's looking me over and could ravish me.

I'm definitely imagining things.

Bristol Greyson hates me.

"Did you want to watch the rest of this cartoon, or should I drive you back?" I ask.

"You can drive me back. I'm ready." She stands and slides her thumb into the tiny pocket on her skirt, and a slip of paper falls to the floor.

I lean down to pick it up. "You dropped—" I glance at it, raising an eyebrow. "Why are you carrying my address with you?"

TEN

BRISTOL

I am dead. I might as well just disappear right now to save myself the humiliation. I slip my shoes on, not answering Liam as he stares at me.

He holds the scrap of paper that I wrote his address on at work.

I had been planning to drop by unannounced and was hoping he'd be glad to see me.

Except I knew he wouldn't be glad.

There'd be zero reason for him to be happy for me to show up, because we hate each other.

Hate isn't even a strong enough word for my feelings toward Liam Moretti.

In middle school, he told everyone that I let him get to third base with me. After that incident, a jock shoved his hand up my skirt in our next class.

I punched the asshole in the throat. Liam looked surprised. I'm not sure if he was more surprised that I got felt up or that I had the balls to punch and silence him.

The next day, the jock came in with a black eye.

Rumor had it that during hockey practice, someone slammed a puck into his face.

I'd like to think that someone did it on purpose.

"The piece of paper with my address, Bristol. You're not getting out of this. What's going on?" He sounds angry, his voice raising an octave as he stands and comes face-to-face with me, but it's more like face-to-chin.

He's a lot taller than I am.

"I just ... I wanted to talk to you."

"Okay." He tilts his head, and his mouth drops. "You showing up at the coffee shop. Have you been stalking me?"

It's Saturday. He's made it a habit of grabbing iced coffee nearly every Saturday between late morning and early afternoon.

I've been watching his habits from the computer system at work. Ariella granted me access to help her with some projects she's working on. A step up from filing.

I may have been taking the research a little too far, doing my own project in secret.

"I wouldn't say stalking." I force a nervous smile and head for the door. Maybe I can just slink out and never speak with him again.

"What would you call it?" He slips on his shoes and follows me as I head outside, hoping to disappear into oblivion.

"This is the first time I've been on your campus." It's definitely the truth. I've never even so much as toured Evergreen University.

I knew when I wanted to attend college, I'd go to Great Falls College. It's a small, private school, much more elite and prestigious.

He shuts the door abruptly behind himself, keys in hand. "I'm driving you home." Unlike earlier, when he was concerned and doting, now he looks pissed.

Honestly, it's the version of Liam I would expect.

"It's fine. I'll take the bus."

"You won't." He points at his piece of shit car and smirks. "I told you not to laugh."

My eyes widen. I'm not sure it'll make it to campus. "You really don't need to drive me home. It's a couple of hours and going to be really long round trip for you."

I'm trying to do him a favor, do us both a favor.

Can we really stand being in the same car together?

Why did I think getting his information and meeting up with him would be a good idea?

He follows my every step, and when I don't head toward his car, he wraps his arm around my waist, guiding me where he wants me.

His breath tickles my ear, sending a shiver down my spine.

I inhale sharply, trying not to let my senses overwhelm me, like earlier. He has a way of doing that to me.

"Tell me again why you have my address in your skirt pocket."

The way his breath caresses my skin fills my stomach with butterflies.

"I was stalking you," I whisper, and my mouth is parched.

He studies me, like he's waiting for me to laugh, but the joke is entirely on me.

My cheeks are hot, and while the sun isn't helping, the flush has to be evident as he glances me over.

"Get in the car, Greyson." He clears his throat, all business, and I step toward the passenger door.

"Are you sure your car is ... safe?" I'm afraid if I open the door and sit in the front seat, I might actually see the pavement beneath my feet.

"I'd never do anything to hurt you, Bristol. You or anyone else—" He's quick to make that clarification.

He waits for me to slide into the passenger seat as he stands outside my car door, leaning in, brooding. He's hot, and his t-shirt rides up just inches, revealing the V between his waistband and navel.

I can't stop staring.

He backs up when he's satisfied that I'm buckled in and slams the door shut.

I exhale sharply, not realizing that I'd been holding my breath, and shut my eyes.

The heat in the car is stifling, and Liam hurries around to climb into the driver's seat and start the engine.

He lowers the windows, letting the heat escape, but it's still stifling. It could also be the heat between us burning me alive.

"You okay?" he asks as I feel the car hum to life and the engine is louder than expected. It's almost like you have to shout over the roar to hear one another, at least with the windows down.

"Fine." I open my eyes and glance at him.

He puts the car in reverse, backs us out of the parking space and pulls onto the main road.

"You can drop me off at the bus station, it's not too late."

"What fun is that when I can hold you hostage for the next couple of hours?"

I laugh at the absurdity and stare at him. His jaw is relaxed, more so than usual. Whenever I'm around him, he's tense and aggravated with me.

I tend to have that effect on him.

"Maybe I should jump out at the next stop sign."

He chuckles under his breath, shaking his head. "You are something else."

"You mean, aside from the enemy?" I can't help but smirk.

I've always hated Liam Moretti. He's a pompous, arrogant jock. Although I despised him long before he started playing hockey.

My hatred for Liam began in the first grade, when he

thought it would be funny to raise my desk into the air with his feet.

I was tiny, and it took nothing for him to make me airborne. A few of the kids behind me were laughing. One of them called me *floater*.

He may not have given me the shitty nickname, but he was responsible for starting the drama.

Never once did he apologize or stop the other kids from bullying me.

I tried ignoring Liam. He kept poking me with his eraser and pulling my pigtails to get my attention.

I went to the teacher, who did nothing about it.

And when I wouldn't give Liam the time of day, he lifted my desk chair once again. So, I got up, and I slugged him.

I left behind a mark.

After that, we were sworn enemies.

Liam nods. "I do recall you throwing a mean right hook."

"You deserved it." I glare at him.

He doesn't answer me.

The silence is overwhelming.

"Are you still bitter that I beat your ass?"

Liam laughs under his breath. "Only because I'd never hit a girl."

We arrive at campus, and I'm expecting Liam to drop me off and leave.

I'm dead wrong.

"What are you doing?" I ask when he parks the car and steps out.

"As long as I'm here, I might as well visit my sister."

Liam is a twin. How do I know this? Because his twin sister, Sophia, and I became inseparable for a few years in grade school through middle school.

By high school, we started having different social circles. She had her friends; I had mine.

There's a tiny bit of bad blood between Sophia and me. Mostly, it's me no longer trusting her.

She killed our friendship.

Freshmen year of high school, she knew that I had this huge crush on Zander Hart. Next week, I find out that he knows, and he's making fun of me. The nickname from the past comes back to haunt me. What a jackass. Needless to say, I never spoke to her again.

I never told Liam what happened. It wasn't like he and I were ever close. I let him believe Sophia, and I just drifted apart. Unless she told him?

"How do you know your sister isn't busy already?"

He taps his temple. "Call it twin intuition."

I roll my eyes and head for the dorms.

Liam is right beside me, like Velcro. "Maybe you should call or text her to make sure she's home."

"Surprises are much more fun." Liam strides right up beside me, his hand falls to my lower back, and I lean into his touch.

I shouldn't.

I should hate him.

I mean, I do hate him, but he stirs weird feelings and emotions in me.

I blame it all on that one ridiculous kiss we shared.

Fiery.

Passionate.

It made my insides throb, and my entire body responded, heart and all.

He'd better not plan on walking me to my dorm room and kissing me again.

"Surprises aren't better." I can't help but think of the surprise visit to my room, and I can admit I was more than a little taken aback by his visit.

But he seemed genuinely surprised it was me answering the door.

Liam isn't that good of an actor.

He can fool his parents and mine, he managed to do that when Sophia and I would go ice skating. Liam was forced to tag along, and he pretended to enjoy spending time with us.

Meanwhile, when they weren't listening or around,

he was threatening to pulverize me. He even shoved rock salt in my ice skates.

"Come with me. I'll prove to you that she'll love the two of us showing up."

"You'll prove to me? Are you willing to make a wager?" I'm joking, but the look on his face says otherwise.

He grins and stops walking, tugging on my hip to draw me toward him.

I suck in an anxious breath as both hands of his touch my bare skin.

I am not turned on by Liam Moretti's touch.

Except, one touch is like a spark that ignites a firestorm.

I press my lips together, trying not to let the embers spark to life. "What, Liam?"

His usual pale-blue eyes darken to a deep blue like the depths of the ocean. He stares at me, the smile never leaving his lips. "If I'm right, you go on a date with me."

My breath catches, and I momentarily forget to breathe.

His fingers caress my hip, which sends my heart racing, and I finally exhale.

“A date with you?” I repeat. It’s insane. “Trust me, you and I would kill each other.” He can’t be serious.

Liam snorts with laughter. “Oh, I know, which I think will make it a million times more fun.”

“Fuck, no.”

“Come on. What’s your bet? What do I have to do if you win?” Liam asks, and the way the pads of his fingers have inched under the hem of my shirt has made my head cloudy.

“You have to do my laundry for a month.”

He raises an eyebrow. “You’re going to make me drive all the way here to do your laundry?”

“Yep!” The smile never leaves my lips. “Every week. I’ll be generous and let you pick the day.”

It’s obvious to me that he’d hate to be dragged out here every week.

"Of course, you'd be the dominant type. You into a little S and M, Greyson?"

"Not in your wildest dreams." Rolling my eyes, I reluctantly pull away from his touch. The sudden coldness spreads over me, but the air is warm, the heat scorching, yet I feel ice cold.

Liam whines. "Come on, admit it. You like the idea of me being your concubine."

"That is so ... wrong." I shake my head. "I didn't ask you to do sexual things for me. Just my laundry! And it's not the least bit funny, Liam."

He smirks and gives me that boyish smile, which makes my heart flutter. "What about your pet?"

"Eww, no." I blanch at the thought of him wearing a collar or drinking from a bowl on the floor. It's weird and definitely not my flavor of kink.

My eyes widen, and I reach for his arm. "Wait. Are you into pet play?"

Liam bends over with laughter, wiping the tears from his eyes. "No, sweetheart. That's not my brand of spice."

I'm relieved, and I'm not even sure why I should care. "What is your brand?" I shouldn't have even asked, but the question slips out before I can stop myself.

He leans closer, his breath tickling my ear. "If you really want to know, maybe you should go out on that hate-date with me."

At least he can admit he hates me. "In your wildest dreams, asshole."

I hurry toward Sophia's dorm room, which is in the building across from mine. We're both freshmen and were randomly assigned our housing and rooms.

I got lucky, my roommate moved out after the first week of classes. Watching *Silence of the Lambs* and *Hannibal* on repeat may have been the trigger. The college never assigned me a new roommate, and now that it's summer, I practically get the entire floor to myself.

Can't complain.

I thrive on silence.

I like the quiet.

It's peaceful. Tranquil. There's no obnoxious music

pouring out from next door or the smell of weed permeating the hallway.

"So, are we on?" Liam asks as I swing open the door and head into her building.

"For the bet?" I step inside first, letting Liam grab the door behind me. I'm not holding it open for him. I refuse to let him think there's so much as a romantic gesture on my end happening, because there's not.

"What else, sweetheart?"

There he goes again, calling me that pervasive nickname.

"I'm not your sweetheart." I glare at him as we enter the elevator together.

He huffs under his breath. "Not yet."

My eyes widen as I turn to face him in the elevator.

"Floor six." Liam gestures for me to hit the button for Sophia's floor.

I press six and glare at him. "What do you mean, *not yet*?" Heat licks my body, flooding every inch of me from head to toe. I can feel my heart race, like it wants to beat outside of my chest. It's overwhelming.

Why does Liam Moretti have this effect on me?

A wry smile spreads across his face. "No reason."

Glaring at him, I shove him farther away. "Keep your distance." It's a warning. I don't need him trying anything, like kissing me.

Not that it wasn't amazing.

But I do not need my heart entangled with him.

He's definitely not the hero.

Not in my story.

Not in anyone's.

Liam Moretti is the villain.

How do I know this?

Because I grew up alongside him at school, and no one changes from villain to hero.

Not in real life.

Only in books or movies.

But this isn't a fairytale, and he's not my Prince Charming. There's no magical transformation waiting to happen here, no grand gesture that will rewrite everything that's come before.

Liam Moretti remains exactly who he's always been —a villain in my life, not a hero, and certainly not the person who will sweep in to save the day.

Liam holds his hands up in surrender. "I haven't done anything." There's that smile and wry grin that makes my stomach do flip-flops. "Sweetheart."

Fuck me, the man is trying to kill me.

Each breath is more pronounced, like gasping for oxygen and having a limited supply. Except I've never been claustrophobic, but the elevator ride is making me dizzy, and I back up against the wall, gripping the handle, using it to keep myself upright.

The room spins, but I refuse to cower to it or admit that I'm quite uncomfortable at the moment. It's not from Liam per se. He hasn't so much as touched me in the confined space.

He watches me, which only makes me more uncomfortable.

I wipe my forehead with the back of my hand, sweat glistening on my skin, and the elevator is suddenly ten degrees warmer. My stomach roils for no reason other than my discomfort.

It's definitely me.

I'm the only one feeling the heat. Liam appears calm and cool.

Another reason to hate him.

I shuffle my feet, my legs feeling a bit like jelly, the railing at my back the only comfort that surrounds me as my vision goes dark.

ELEVEN

LIAM

While the ride up to Sophia's room in the elevator is a bit tense, just watching Bristol is entertaining.

Until it's not.

She sweats profusely.

I assumed it was because she's thinking about me in some carnal way, fantasizing about the two of us together.

I've had my fair share of Bristol fantasies, but it usually gets cut short when she's chasing me with a dagger, an axe, any type of weapon, really, wearing a bikini, or nothing at all.

But when I watch her eyes roll back in her head, I dash across the small space and catch her on her descent before she can hit the floor.

The girl fainted.

"Bristol." I can feel her breathing as I scoop her up into my arms.

The elevator dings, and we reach the sixth floor. I step out, carrying Bristol, and stalk down to my sister's room.

Sophia had better be home.

This is going to be one hell of a surprise, and not the good kind.

Bristol's eyes open, they're heavy, and she's gasping for air, like she's been competing in a triathlon. "What—"

"You passed out in the elevator." I hurriedly make my way to Sophia's door.

If she's not home, I'll have to carry her across campus to her dorm.

She's really going to hate me, more than she already does.

“Put me down,” Bristol says, but her voice doesn’t hold the normal conviction.

I ignore Bristol and knock on the door with my left foot, trying to get my sister’s attention if she’s home. “Sophia. Open up!” My shout is louder than my knock-kick.

There is rustling and movement. The dorm room door opens, and her eyes widen.

“Bristol passed out in the elevator.” I brush past Sophia, letting myself into the room and place Bristol on the bed, not asking my sister’s permission. I know she’d understand.

“Should we call an ambulance?” Sophia glances from me to Bristol.

“I’m fine. Really, there’s no reason to overreact.” She forces a smile, but her body trembles as she brings her knees toward her chest and bends them but continues lying flat on her back.

“This isn’t an overreaction.” I’m truly worried about her. I never thought I’d see the day where I’d care what happened to Bristol Greyson.

Her humiliating me when we were six was enough to make me despise her. I had flirted with her, and she punched me in the face!

I may not have been a great flirt in the first grade; I was just trying to get her attention.

Make her notice me.

She noticed me all right.

She spewed nonsense and told me I was chunky.

I was a bit on the chubby side when I was six. It wasn't until puberty, I gained some height and filled out, but she didn't have to point out my flaws.

And when I called her mean, she hit me.

Talk about getting laughed at because I was "hit by a girl" and, yes, embarrassingly enough, I cried.

I tried like hell not to cry, but the girl was brutal, and I was young, unable to control my emotions.

My dad wasn't pleased that I got hit by a girl. I kept the part where I cried a secret. The teacher only saw bits and pieces, and what got reported was only half the story. I never bothered to speak up and give my side.

Dad wouldn't have approved or been pleased with me crying in front of the other kids.

It was bad enough that I was humiliated and laughed at by the other boys in my class. I didn't need to relive it in front of the principal, or worse, when our parents came to a meeting, or again, when we were forced to have dinner at the Greyson's home.

Bristol Greyson was a menace.

After that, I vowed never to catch feelings for her again.

But what I'm feeling right now aren't those kinds of feelings, I'm concerned about her passing out in the elevator.

It's not normal.

Sure, Bristol isn't exactly a normal girl, but I'm also not a jackass. I wasn't raised to walk away from trouble, either.

I can thank Mom for that, she's always been a bit of a badass. Not that my father hasn't been, he runs the Italian mafia in New York City. But I've always been closer with my mother. Probably because she raised me.

I hadn't even met my father until I was in preschool.

"I faint all the time. It's just ... the heat." She waves a hand dismissively, and I can't help but witness her small body tremors as she inhales and exhales quite loudly.

Sophia grabs a chair, pulling it up beside me. "Sit."

I sit beside the bed, reaching for Bristol's hand. "What do you mean, you faint all the time?"

I haven't even so much as started medical school. While I know I want to be a doctor, I'm in over my head for helping her.

"It's nothing. Really. Please don't look at me like I'm dying, because I'm not that lucky." She forces a smile, but I don't return the sentiment.

"I'm worried about you." I glance back at Sophia, who is standing watching us. She's silent, smart enough to know not to intervene.

"Don't be. You never were before today." Bristol glares at me like I'm the reason for what happened, when I, instead, kept her from hitting the ground.

She's right, but we've both been awful to each other in the past.

I'm not sure why I even offered her a ride home.

That's not true.

That kiss she stole a few months ago, I can't stop thinking about it.

Her lips.

The taste of her mouth on mine.

The feel of her breath against my cheek.

The way her tongue felt when it slipped into my mouth.

Every part of me hums to life just thinking about that kiss.

My body responded in ways I've never felt, from what should be described as a simple kiss.

That was before she deepened it. Or maybe I was the one who pulled her closer.

I can still smell her perfume.

Although now I don't have to imagine her perfect scent, I'm right next to her. I just have to be careful not to take a huge whiff, or I might seem crazy.

I'm not obsessed with the enemy, Bristol Greyson.

Not even I believe that silent mantra that itches my head.

"Quit staring, Moretti, I'm fine."

I can't blame her for using my last name, since I've been calling her Greyson.

I hate feeling that there's a spark between us. Anyone else, and I'd be excited, elated even, but with Bristol, I'm just waiting for her to rip out my heart and stomp all over it.

"Have you seen a doctor about the fainting?"

Her eyes tighten. "It's none of your business." She's pissed once again. Not a huge surprise, considering who's angry with me.

I've gotten used to her hatred of me. It's not like I see her very often anymore. That was one reason I chose not to attend Great Falls University. I heard Bristol Greyson was attending; I opted for somewhere far away from her.

I'd never admit that little fact to anyone. Not even my twin knows the reason I picked Evergreen University.

Plus, the scholarship was an added bonus. Dad was surprisingly thrilled that I picked EU, which I thought was a little weird.

Mom always had more interest in hockey, at least attending my high school games. I can't recall Dad ever going to a high school game that I played, but he's always busy with work.

I never really cared.

Playing hockey was about having fun.

And getting a full-ride scholarship and guaranteeing me a spot on the hockey team with Ashton and Luca, it sealed the deal for me.

While I'd met them when we were much younger, it was the fact that I'd seen Luca play against the Predators the previous year, when we toured the campus.

I wanted to be on his team.

He's a fantastic center.

I play right wing.

We make an amazing combination, and I wouldn't be that far away from my twin sister. Going out of state was going to be a huge adjustment for Sophia. I felt a little bad that I wasn't going to attend Great Falls with her, but knowing we were a couple of hours apart, it was perfect.

Sophia steps closer, glancing Bristol over. "Can I get you anything? Water? Juice?"

"Do you have anything salty? And water would be good."

Sophia grabs a bottle of water from her mini-fridge. "We have potato chips and pretzels."

Bristol reaches for her small satchel purse and retrieves a packet of electrolyte mix. "Can you pour this in for me?"

I take the packet from her trembling hand, open the water bottle, tear open the packet, and pour it inside.

I secure the lid, shaking the bottle, letting the drink mix thoroughly.

"The potato chips should have more salt."

Sophia hands Bristol a single serving sized bag of potato chips.

Bristol opens the bag of chips and retrieves a tiny salt packet that she probably stole from a restaurant and tears the packet over the chips.

My eyes widen at the amount of salt she's consuming.

"Are you sure you're not flooding your system with so much salt you're passing out?"

Bristol glares at me and snarls, "I have low blood pressure."

"Oh." Well, fuck me. I feel like a dumbass. I'm so screwed when I eventually start my classes for medical school.

My silence invites her to speak more about it, which surprises me.

"I've been this way since I was thirteen." I don't remember Bristol fainting in school, but we had only a handful of classes together as teens.

"Cute. Stubborn. Causing all sorts of trouble?" I joke, trying to alleviate her concerns.

Her brow pinches. "You think I'm cute?" She moves to sit up, and I'm right there, putting pillows behind her in case she falls.

I don't say anything.

She sits up and unscrews the water bottle cap. It takes two hands for her to hold the electrolyte drink, her hands shaking profusely as she dips her head back and takes a sip.

I want to help her, but I might get my head chewed off and screamed at.

I'm not that six-year-old boy anymore.

If she gives me shit, I'm not afraid to dish it back.

I help her steady the water bottle, and she takes another swig.

"You don't have to—"

"I want to," I interrupt her. "So, you pass out a lot?"

She takes another sip and then hands me the bottle. "Can you put the lid back on?"

I take the lid and bottle and secure it for her. She lies back down and momentarily closes her eyes.

"I'm sorry, Sophia, I didn't mean to ruin your Saturday." Bristol's eyes flicker open, and she stares at me. There's a strange, unfamiliar gaze that crosses her features. It's not something I recognize or have seen before.

I try not to let her unintentionally get into my head.

"Don't apologize." Sophia grabs a seat on the edge of the unoccupied bed on the opposite wall. "It's nice to have company who isn't reading all day and telling me to shush. I like a good book too, but I also need some socialization."

Sophia shares a room, even during the summer, which is unusual.

Most kids go home during the summer, but Sophia and I have no desire to return to Antonio. Not that we don't love the man—he is our father—but there's too much business going on at home. Not enough ... fun.

And I prefer the parties and girls.

Sophia's roommate has books stacked against the wall, and she even secured a floating bookshelf, displaying several more novels.

The difference between sides is quite stunning. Sophia's side is riddled with dragons and fairies.

My sister loves fantasy. Especially romantasy.

Sophia has been on a dragons kick lately. Two years ago, it was everything fey. The posters on display hang on her side of the room with dragons in blue, gold, black, a huge array of colors that I never even considered existing.

I always thought dragons were gray, dark, more like dinosaurs, just had wings and breathed fire.

Thankfully, I won't run into any dragons, unless you consider fire-breather Bristol Greyson to be a dragon. That girl could set fire to a room with just a single look.

But right now, she's anything but that fiery girl I'm used to dealing with and hating.

She's vulnerable, and I'm not used to seeing her like that or being around her.

It's a bit unsettling.

"You don't have to stay and watch over me. I'm okay. I'll go back to my room in a minute." Bristol sits up and reaches for the water bottle that I've been holding.

I unscrew the lid for her, and she uses two hands to

grab it, managing a little easier to take a sip since the drink isn't full.

She takes another swig and then glances at me. "Really, you can leave."

I smirk and glance at my sister. "Did we manage to surprise you?"

Sophia nods her head. "Yes, but worst surprise ever! I'm glad Bristol is all right, but you carrying her at my door was not something I expected to see—ever."

"So, you're not glad to see us?" I need to turn this around quickly, so I'm not the one losing the bet with Bristol.

"Of course, I'm glad to see you! I always like when my brother comes to visit." Sophia stands and stretches. "Are you sure I can't do anything else for you? Do you want me to call your dad?"

Bristol's eyes widen in horror. "No!"

Her outburst stuns me for a moment. Shock wrestles through my veins, expecting her to use her father whenever she damn well pleases. He is a billionaire and the owner of the NHL team, the Ice Dragons.

It's the card she always managed to play in school when something didn't go her way.

Spoiled brat.

"Okay. And you don't need a doctor? I'm just worried about you going back to your room and being alone. You can hang with me." Sophia gestures to the room. "I'm not really doing much of anything. I was thinking of putting on a movie."

"A movie sounds good." Bristol grabs a few potato chips that are coated in extra salt and munches on them.

She's no longer clammy and covered in sweat. The normal color has returned to her cheeks. If it weren't for the tremors, I wouldn't even know anything is wrong.

I feel bad leaving, but it is a little over a two-hour drive to get home.

"What are you going to watch?"

Their movie choice could very much make that decision for me.

"*You've Got Mail*," Sophia says, and grabs the disc

from her collection and puts it into the Blu-ray player.

“That’s an old one.” I’d seen it once, years ago. It’s a romance, not exactly what I’d be choosing to watch.

“I’ve never seen it.” Bristol settles back on the bed and adjusts the pillows, making herself more comfortable.

“You’ve never seen it?” Sophia’s eyes widen. “Oh my gosh! It has the classic enemies-to-lovers trope. It’s one of my favorites. Do you want me to make some microwave popcorn?”

“Yes!” Bristol’s eyes light up. “That sounds perfect.”

“I’m going to bail.” I would hang out if it was a movie I have any interest in watching. A chick flick is definitely not one of those movies.

“Are you sure? I can make room on the bed.” Bristol shifts over on the mattress, practically against the wall, leaving me half the bed to lie with her. “Come join me.”

TWELVE

ASHTON

Earlier that morning...

The morning light barely streams in, but Nova is awake. Her fingers glide across my skin, making my heart flutter and my cock stir.

"Morning," she whispers, and her mouth is next to my ear, her breath sending shivers across my body in waves. I pull her above me, loving the feeling of her body nestled against mine.

"You're up early." I fight a yawn. "Why are we up early?" I ask. There's no early morning practice. I'll head to the gym later in the afternoon with the guys.

She straddles my waist, her fingers dance across my chest, but her eyes are on my skin.

I lift her chin, wanting to know what's got her frazzled.

I know Nova well enough to see that she didn't sleep well if she's up at this hour. Something is troubling her.

"I'm worried about Harper."

Harper.

That wasn't exactly what I was expecting to hear from her lips.

Nova climbs off my body, lying beside me, her fingers on my arm. "She told me about the creepy guy at the grocery store."

I exhale through my nose.

We made Liam swear not to tell Nova, but no one could keep Harper from saying anything.

"It's Dante, isn't it?" Nova asks.

Do I lie to Nova? Tell her it's Dante, to protect her and Harper from a harsher truth?

"You know I can't talk about the job." I pull Nova against me, my arms wrapping around her body, and she drapes a leg over mine.

"Sometimes I hate that you work for him."

"Dante?" I guess.

Nova nods.

It's not a conversation that we've ever shared before.

"I didn't know that," I say, unsure how to feel. It's not a surprise to her, I've been working for Dante for months, long before the two of us first hooked up.

"I just, I wish we could be something other than our parents." Nova sighs and sits up in bed, pulling the covers around herself.

She's naked, and while I'd rather see all of her, I'll settle for a glimpse here and there.

I follow her motions, sitting up with her, grabbing a pillow and using it against the wall for support. "We're not our parents. And even if we were, are Moreno and Paige so terrible?" I ask, wondering what she thinks of her family.

Unlike Luca, who despises Dante, I never got that same feeling from Nova regarding her parents.

"Mom is wonderful. My father, on the other hand, he can be a bit of an ass." Nova is blunt and pulls her knees up to her chest. "I know I'm lucky. I have everything anyone could ever want—a house, clothing, food, my tuition paid for, but it's all blood money."

"Blood money?" I smile. "Dante isn't the worst monster out there. He's just a man."

"A man who kills people for a living." Nova is well aware of the chain of command; he may be the mafia boss, but he doesn't typically get his hands dirty.

She wraps her arms around her legs, her chin resting on her knees.

"I just wish we could get away from all of it." She turns her head, staring at me. "I'm worried about Harper and Zeke. Whoever that man was, threats like that, they don't just disappear unless they're meant to scare. Dante doesn't just scare people."

I purse my lips, and her gaze tightens.

"What is it?" Nova asks, her hand reaching out for mine. "You're keeping a secret. I see it in that look on your face."

I hate how easily she's learned to read me.

"It's nothing."

She sighs and lies back down, stretching out beneath the covers, pulling the blankets up around herself. Nova rolls onto her side, facing away from me.

"You're mad." Her body language screams that she's pissed at me, but her silence is what bothers me more.

Nova emits a heavy sigh and rolls around to face me. "I wish you'd trust me to tell me the truth. If Harper is in danger, I want to help."

"I don't want you getting hurt." I pull her against me, wanting to touch her, caress her, prove to her that I do care about her, above all else.

"I can look after myself. I carry a stun gun and pepper spray with me, and I know how to use a gun."

I roll Nova onto her back, guiding her legs apart with my knee, and she bites down on her bottom lip, smiling up at me.

"You don't get to use sex to avoid the conversation."

"So then, let's talk," I whisper against her neck. I drop featherlight kisses across her skin.

Her breathing becomes heavier and more pronounced as I trail a path down and across her breasts.

"I'm glad you know how to stay safe." I run my tongue over her nipple, and her body arches into my touch.

"Ashton," she moans, and her fingers tangle in my hair.

I love it when she touches me. Her fingers send tingles through my body. "I just want to protect you." My kisses move down and across her stomach, and I feel her sharp intake of breath.

"Be honest with me." Nova struggles to keep her eyes open.

"Always." I wish it were that simple. I'm not lying to her, just keeping dangerous secrets from her.

I'm protecting her.

Protecting the family.

I descend farther on her body and tease her with my breath between her thighs.

"Ashton," her voice comes out desperate, and the smile grows on my face. I love hearing that sound, listening to her both needy and eager for me.

I silence all further thoughts from her mind as I drag my tongue over her pussy and she's moaning and quivering, her fingers tangling in the bedsheets.

I love the sounds she makes, the pleas and moans that spill from her lips.

She's never quiet, at least not anymore.

Her moans make my cock rock hard, and I crave the yearning to fuck her. But not yet.

It's about her pleasure.

I let my tongue tease her folds, and she whimpers. The sound is pure heaven.

My tongue darts out around her little pink pearl, listening to each moan and feeling her body tremble as she grows closer.

Her skin is flushed, her breathing thicker, and she struggles to keep her eyes open.

My fingers slide inside her pussy, and her back arches off the mattress.

"You taste so fucking good," I moan and love the reaction it entices.

Her insides clench down onto my fingers as I tease her and thrust, stretching her, until I find that sweet spot and repeat the gesture as her eyes slam shut.

Oh yeah, she's fucking close.

"Fuck, Ashton!"

Pride beams inside of me, knowing that I can make her come.

Her back arches off the mattress, and it takes everything inside of me to keep watching.

Desire mounts within me, wanting to pin her down and fuck her, because my cock is pulsating, but I resist the urge.

Her body trembles, and the moan that courses through her is pure bliss as she chases the orgasm.

I can't stop smiling, my fingers and lips grazing over every inch of skin as I climb back up her body, marking her with my lips. I can't get enough of *her*.

She's mine.

I'm hers.

The rest of the world doesn't matter, so long as we're together.

Her eyes lazily open, a smile tugging at the corners. "I may actually be able to fall asleep."

Her soft mumble is sweet, but I have other ideas if she's still up for it.

"Fall asleep?" I tease, whining at her. "Come on, it's my turn." I'd let her sleep if that's what she needs, but I always love the banter and what it leads to with her.

"You didn't let me finish my sentence. I may be able to fall asleep after two or three more rounds." She grins and pounces on me, making me the happiest man alive.

My fingers rake over her back, watching as Nova sleeps beside me.

We've spent the past several hours curled in bed together, not that there was much sleeping involved.

I love summer.

No school. No classes. Just fun.

She pulls the covers up over her head as the afternoon light pours in through the curtains.

"Sleep, babe." I drop a kiss on her shoulder.

I dozed off for a few minutes after our early morning bedroom festivities, but I skipped breakfast and lunch. We were too busy wrapped up in each other.

I'm famished.

Nova has a habit of burning up all of my calories and then some.

I slip out of bed, get dressed and quietly head out of Nova's bedroom. At least we don't have to hide our relationship anymore. I'm glad Luca found out. Not that it couldn't have been smoother or anything, because being worried about him chopping off my dick while sleeping was a real fear unlocked.

We're over it.

At least he's over it.

I slip into the kitchen, glancing in the fridge for something I can eat before dinner.

My stomach grumbles, and little Zeke comes toddling in, wrapping his arms around my legs, holding on tight before leaning back.

The kid would do well in acrobatics. I've seen him climb Luca like a jungle gym.

"Hey, kiddo." I ruffle his hair and then grab some lunchmeat from the fridge. I make myself a sandwich, and Zeke points at the turkey breast.

"Turkey tunnel." Zeke points again when I don't give him anything fast enough.

Harper approaches from around the corner of the kitchen and grabs Zeke, lifting him into her arms. "You're getting too big for this."

"Turkey tunnel," he repeats and points at my sandwich.

"Can I give him one?" I ask, checking with Harper.

"Sure."

I grab a slice of turkey and roll it up, offering Zeke a turkey tunnel. He grabs it from my hands and chomps down with a grin. The kid loves bread if it's a roll or toast, but try to put meat on his sandwich and he sounds like he's being murdered.

I watch from the counter, taking a bite of my sandwich, and my stomach grumbles, like I'm not feeding it fast enough.

"Where's Nova?" Harper puts Zeke down the minute he begins squirming in her arms.

As much as he likes to be carried, he prefers to have free rein over the house.

"Taking a nap."

Zeke tears out of the kitchen, running around like a little maniac. The kid has tons of energy. "I'm going to take him for a walk and meet Kensley at the park. I'll catch you later."

My eyes widen, and I quickly finish the last of my lunch, shoving it into my mouth and chewing quickly as I follow to grab my shoes.

"I'll come with you."

"You want to go with us on a walk?" Harper eyes me skeptically.

"Sure, I could use some sunlight. Just give me a minute," I say and hurry to my bedroom to make sure that I'm packing heat, in case anything goes down.

The gun is concealed under my shirt. The last thing I need is Harper asking questions or Zeke pointing it out.

Ten minutes later, we're walking along the sidewalk. My gaze is casually darting around, keeping an eye out to make sure we're not being watched or followed.

"I'm surprised you decided to join us," Harper says. "If you weren't dating Nova, I'd swear you had a thing for Kensley."

"Your friend is cute, but she really isn't my type."

"Your type is Nova, we all know." Harper smiles and shakes her head.

Zeke runs alongside us. I stick to the outside, walking near the street, in case any cars come up, and I can also protect Zeke if he darts onto the road.

He hasn't yet, but he makes me nervous as he runs

back and forth. I swear the kid is in a game of chase with himself.

From across the main road, Kensley is walking with Brooks.

“I think you may have a little competition,” I joke, nudging Harper.

“Since when did they start dating?” Harper glares at me, like I’ve been keeping her best friend’s secret this entire time.

News flash: I don’t pay attention to who Kensley or any of my teammates are dating. Unless they’re flirting with Nova, in which case I’d be forced to rearrange their faces.

“Beats me.” I chase after Zeke, pretending to be a zombie as he runs and squeals, giggling as he tries to get away from me.

As he nears the end of the sidewalk, I scoop him up, grabbing him so he can’t run onto the road.

“Gosh! Zombie Ashton is super scary!” Kensley teases as she and Brooks catch up with us.

Brooks whispers something to Kensley, but I don’t eavesdrop or particularly care.

I trust Brooks around Harper, and I know Kensley is safe. She's had a thorough vetting and background check, especially after her knowledge of Dante's business dealings.

We've also tapped her phone, and she's been squeaky clean, keeping our secrets. That's more than I can say about Harper, who told Kensley about the mafia.

She's lucky she's married to Luca, because Dante isn't a forgiving man.

I let them walk ahead of us with Harper while I stay in the back, giving Zeke a piggyback ride.

I'm on heightened alert as we near the playground, the same park where Harper had first seen one of DeLuca's men.

There are a few kids playing, moms and dads hanging out, watching their children. No one who seems out of the ordinary.

"Down!" Zeke squeals after we cross the street, and I carefully maneuver him off my shoulders and let him tear off.

I keep my gaze on Zeke as well as constantly doing surveillance, making sure no one is walking or driving by who seems suspicious.

Harper and Kensley grab a seat on the bench. I stand a few feet away, giving the girls some privacy to talk.

Besides, I don't need to hear their gossip or about Kensley and Brooks' love life.

No, thank you.

Brooks wanders over to me, clearly bored. "You look tense," he says, staring at me.

"Just keeping an eye on Zeke."

"Isn't that Luca's job or Harper's?" Brooks glances back at the girls behind him.

I have the best vantage point, giving me a clear line of sight of the girls and Zeke, while also watching most of the road.

"He's my best friend's kid."

"I didn't mean to offend," Brooks is quick to make amends. "I'm just surprised you chose to spend your afternoon with Harper."

"We're friends." Brooks has no idea about the mafia, the threats, the danger that we're constantly under. I force a smile. "I thought she shouldn't walk alone to the park."

"It's the afternoon," Brooks says, and then his eyes widen. "Oh—that's right. I did hear about the incident at the grocery store from Kensley."

I'm not surprised that Harper shared what happened with her best friend.

My phone buzzes. I grab it from my pocket and notice it's Luca.

"Hello."

"Please tell me you have eyes on my wife and son." Luca sounds slightly out of breath.

"We're at the park with Kensley and Brooks. You're welcome to join us." I force a smile as Brooks watches me intently.

"I'll be there soon."

I end the call and slide my phone back into my pocket.

"So, did you guys call the cops?" Brooks asks.

"What?" I'm not sure what he's talking about, but whatever it involves, no, we didn't call the fucking police.

"When Harper and Zeke were harassed by that weird guy. Did you guys go to the cops about it?"

"No." I glance from Brooks to Harper.

I don't like where this line of questioning is heading.

"Why not?" Brooks doesn't back down. "I mean, you should go to the police. The way Kensley talked, Harper was worried about getting kidnapped or something. Maybe it's nothing, but at least they could investigate."

"Leave it alone, would you?" I walk toward the girls, hoping Brooks will get the hint and change the subject.

"I'm just concerned—" Brooks continues and follows me as I stand beside Harper.

"Concerned about what?" Kensley asks, overhearing the conversation on our approach.

"If there was footage of the guy who harassed Harper, why didn't anyone take it to the police department? You should file a report. If he's threatening Harper, then he's probably doing the same to other women out there." Brooks is trying to be helpful, but he's really *not* helping the situation.

Harper's brow pinches, and she glances up at me. "I know something's going on with you and Luca."

"There's nothing going on. I promise, my romantic feelings are one-hundred-percent toward Nova."

Harper snorts and shakes her head. "You know that's not what I'm talking about."

"What are you talking about?" I meet her intense stare.

She's not foolish enough to mention Dante or the mafia in front of Brooks. And while Kensley is aware that Dante runs the mafia, she doesn't need to know any more information. She knows too much as it is.

Harper stands, grabs my arm and drags me several feet away from her friends. "You and Luca are keeping secrets—about something. I understand what you do with Dante, your work, is private, but when it spills over into my life or my son's, we have a problem."

A faint smile tugs at the corner of my lips. "Are you threatening me, Harper?"

"Whatever you've gotten Luca involved in, so help me, if he ends up hurt or something happens to my son, I will hold you and Dante personally responsible."

"Understood." I glance past Harper and force a smile, relieved Luca is here. He can deal with his wife, Brooks, and the plethora of questions that seem to be surfacing. It's his problem now.

THIRTEEN

BRISTOL

I offer Liam the chance to climb into bed with me. It's not an intimate gesture; we're watching a movie in Sophia's dorm room.

But it feels intimate when he rises from the chair and moves to the bed, sitting down.

My heart palpitates in my chest as I keep my hands to myself.

Liam has been a pain in my ass all my life.

I'm not about to start falling for him because we're sharing a bed ... we're not even sleeping in it.

I don't move, lying perfectly still. I feel awkward as Liam stretches out and makes himself comfortable.

He raises his arm and puts it behind his head. Everything about him is huge. He takes up more than half the mattress, although I don't believe it's intentional.

The extra-long, twin-sized mattress is still tight for two. I'm still trembling, and he glances at me.

Can he feel it on the mattress?

"Do you want me to get you a blanket?" Liam offers.

Sophia microwaves popcorn for all of us before we start the movie.

"Do you mind if I crawl under the covers?" I ask Sophia.

"Go for it. Just don't do anything nasty with that one." She points at her brother.

"Don't worry. I'm not interested in catching cooties." While I'm joking around, I'm also serious about what the hell Liam may have caught with other girls.

He seems like the player type.

Probably because I've been around hockey players all my life, professional ones. While my father has always been loyal to Emerson, there were some players I heard stories about and their sexual prowess.

Dad tried to keep those guys out of the house when he'd have his buddies over, when I was younger. As I grew up, I saw and heard more, understood quite a bit of what was happening around me.

Emerson insisted that the parties had to be someplace else.

I'll admit, I was disappointed, because some of the players were easy on the eyes.

Although Liam has all of them beat, with his thick, golden hair and eyes the color of the Caribbean Sea. The clear blue has flecks of gold and shimmers like turquoise under the sun.

I'll bet he gets asked quite often if he's wearing colored contacts, because his eyes are that captivating.

No doubt, he's aware he's got the looks and the athlete's body.

Another reason to hate him.

He gets the girls, all of them, begging to date him.

I'm sure of it.

Sophia brings over a bag of popcorn and hands it to me. "Are you two willing to share, or do I need to make another bag?"

Liam nudges me, and I glare at him for touching me. I have a feeling he's going to make this entire movie unbearable.

Why did I invite him to lie next to me?

What the hell was I thinking?

"I can share if she doesn't hog all the popcorn or pour gallons of salt in the bag."

"That's the best way to eat it."

Sophia rolls her eyes. "I'll make you a bag, Liam."

She puts another one in the microwave, and we wait to start the movie because there's no way we'd hear the dialogue over the loud noise.

I dip my hand into the bag and grab a piece, taking a bite. "Definitely needs more salt." I grab another salt packet buried away in my purse and pour it into the popcorn bag. I close the top, shake it up and then try another piece. "Gosh, that's great."

Liam wrinkles his nose. "You like to eat seawater?"

"No, and that would be drinking." I elbow him, and he pretends like I injured him.

"Oof. You've got an arm on you." His brow grimaces, and he's pouting and seems a bit over-the-top to me.

Just like when we were kids.

"Oh, come on, Mr. Hotshot Hockey, no way that hurt." I've seen him get swung at and assaulted by far more violent men on the ice when he played against the Predators.

Liam grins and reaches for my bag of popcorn. "You owe me a taste for that brutal beating."

"You are so overly dramatic!"

I reach my hand into the popcorn bag and toss a few pieces at his face.

He tries to catch them with his mouth but fails miserably. It's almost ... cute.

But I refuse to ever refer to Liam Moretti as cute.

Liam picks up the individual pieces of popcorn and brings them to his lips.

I can't help but stare. Every movement he makes stirs something deep within me.

Damn him.

It must be on purpose. The way his eyes make my stomach fall to the floor, and that smile.

Oh, that cocky grin that stares right through me and makes my insides tingle.

"Me, dramatic?" Liam smiles as he nibbles on one piece at a time.

I can tell by his face that it's too salty, but he pretends like he's enjoying every piece. He reaches for my bag, and I raise an eyebrow. There's no way he wants more.

"If you like salty snacks, I may know another tasty treat for you..."

My eyes widen, and I smack him hard on the arm. "Eww, gross! You're such a perv."

The sound of kernels popping drowns out our conversation from Sophia. She doesn't seem to notice what transpires until she pulls the bag out of the microwave.

"You two got weirdly quiet." Sophia opens the bag, and steam wafts out from the top.

"Careful." He climbs off the bed and grabs the bag from Sophia before she has a chance to burn herself.

"Thanks." Sophia puts a third bag into the microwave, and already I miss Liam sitting next to me.

The bed feels cold and lonely.

What the hell is wrong with me?

Maybe I hit my head when I fainted.

A moment later, he's back on the bed, and instantly, I relax. It's honestly not the reaction I was expecting from myself. Being around Liam usually riles me up. I've always hated him. There's zero chance I'll start catching feelings for him.

But maybe he's not entirely bad.

Just a little pain in my ass bad.

"You're quiet. Are you feeling all right?" Liam rests a hand on my thigh as he places his bag of popcorn on the bed and leans it against his knees to keep it from spilling. "Do you need more salt?" There's a wicked grin that crosses his face, like he's joking.

"Do you have a salt shaker handy?"

Liam pauses and shakes his head. "Nope, I'll have to steal one from the dining hall for you."

"That's all right. I think there's enough salt on my popcorn." I nudge his leg with my knee, and his popcorn bag topples over, but luckily, only a handful of pieces spill out.

He grabs the wayward pieces, eating them first, and glares at me. "That was on purpose." There's a menacing tone to his voice; it's more than just annoyance, almost a growl.

"Damn right it was. You suggested I suck your cock earlier."

"What?" Sophia's eyes widen, and she coughs. "When the hell was that comment?"

"I didn't say for her to suck my dick," Liam says. "What I told her was—"

Sophia holds up a hand to stop him from finishing his next sentence. "We may be twins, but there are some things that we don't need to share."

I can't help but laugh, and Liam glares at me. It's playful, heated, and makes me flustered.

He should not be making me feel *that* way.

Thankfully, Sophia turns the movie on, and Liam doesn't say another word. He shuffles slightly on the bed, trying to make himself comfortable.

I glance at him from the corner of my eye.

He's the biggest distraction.

It's hard to focus on the movie when Liam is in bed with me.

Not that we're doing anything sexual.

I'd rather cut off my own arm or leg.

Maybe I'm the one a tad dramatic.

It's Liam. The same guy who, in high school senior year, slept with two juniors who were best friends.

He dated both of them at the same time, without the other's knowledge, until it fell apart.

Not even a hint of remorse.

I'm not about to give him my heart when I know he'll stomp all over it.

Liam glances at me, and I dart my gaze back to the television.

He laughs under his breath.

"What?" Sophia asks. "That scene isn't funny."

"No, but the one right next to me is hilarious." Liam grins, and I'm trying my damndest to stare straight ahead, but I'm feeling a bit flushed with his gaze on me.

Turning my head, I glare at him. "What's so funny, Moretti?"

"You hauled up right next to that wall like you're going to fuck it." His voice is low and rough and sends a shiver down my spine.

My mouth goes dry, and my lips part with a slight gasp. "You've stolen all the bed! Where else am I supposed to lie?"

"You can share my bed." Sophia is across the room and pauses the movie since clearly none of us are paying attention to the film.

Liam glares at his sister, a knowing smile playing on his lips. "You'd like that, wouldn't you, little sis?"

"Little, I'm two minutes younger than you." Sophia's glaring at her brother, and I swear they wear the same snarl.

It's uncanny.

"Yeah, but you're six inches shorter." There's that cocky smile again, and I really want to wipe it off his face.

"Would you rather I scoot closer?" I bury the nerves surfacing and ignore the pounding in my chest as I practically climb on Liam, draping a leg over his, my hand finding his chest.

If he wants to be flirty, two can play at that game.

I can feel the steady rhythm of his heart.

It's beating fast, but nowhere near as quick as mine.

Liam growls at me, an arm sliding out and circling my waist. "What are you doing?"

"What am I doing?" my voice squeaks, betraying me. I clear my throat, hoping he doesn't notice, but that would be impossible. Maybe he just won't say anything about it. "What are you doing?" I push the question onto him, my gaze meeting his.

I refuse to cower or to let Liam have the upper hand.

In one swift motion, he has his hands on my hips and pulls me across his leg and has me nestled between his thighs.

I'm curled on my side, my body resting against his chest. I feel the rise and fall of his chest, every heartbeat, even the heat of his breath against my hair as I swear, he plants a kiss to my forehead.

"Did you just kiss me?" I choke out, and this game may be fun, but it's stressing me out. My heart is galloping in my chest, and my fingers move to his thigh, trembling, as the adrenaline surge assaults me yet again.

Liam's breath is warm, and he exhales deeply, his strong arms wrapped around me. "Watch the movie, Firebreather."

I snort at his nickname for me.

"Firebreather?"

Liam shrugs and smiles. "Am I wrong?"

Sophia chimes in with a laugh. "I mean, that could describe either one of you when you're together."

"I picked it first!" Liam scoots back slightly against the wall, his arms around me, pulling me to lie with him against his chest.

I shift so that I see the movie better, lying flush against his back, his arms encircling my hips.

It's intimate, the way he holds me in his arms.

His little nickname stirs something buried deep inside of me.

I don't hate it.

Not that I'd ever tell Liam, or he'd never let me live it down.

Just like being in his strong arms, his back against me, curled up, it isn't so bad.

I try to focus on the movie, but all I can feel is each breath that he takes. It's slow, even, steady.

How is he not panicking right now?

How can the man who hates me hold me like it's no big deal and focus on the movie in front of us?

He rests his chin on the top of my head, and I wiggle against him, not wanting him to do that.

Liam clears his throat and shifts slightly.

Did I inadvertently make him uncomfortable?

His arms wrap around my waist, holding me against his chest. His touch on my arms is soft, gentle, comforting.

I'm exhausted after the fainting spell, and I struggle to keep my eyes open.

The pads of his fingers dance from my arms to my stomach, and it lulls me to sleep.

I awaken as the credits roll and I'm half tucked in the crook of one of Liam's arms, holding my neck up.

My eyes flutter open, and I pull away, glancing back at him to see that he's used pillows to prop up his arm, for me.

There's no way he was in the position for his benefit.

"Sorry I fell asleep."

"It's all right, Firebreather." The way he says that nickname sends warmth tingling through my body. "Next time, just don't drool on me."

My eyes widen in horror. "I don't drool in my sleep!"

Liam chuckles. "Tell that to your lips."

Glaring at him, I crawl away, scooting off the bed. "Thanks for the movie, Sophia. I should head back to my room."

Liam climbs off the bed behind me. "I ought to head back to campus."

He's got quite a drive ahead of him.

"Thanks again for driving me home." I still can't believe he offered to drive me instead of making me take the bus.

This nice-guy routine is really throwing me.

But then again, he tosses in a jab at me about drooling in my sleep, which I'm confident never happened, and he irks me again.

"I'll walk you back to your dorm."

"That isn't necessary. You've got a long drive; you should just head out." I slip my shoes on and grab the empty bag of popcorn, tossing it into the trash.

I give Sophia an awkward hug goodbye and step out into the hallway, Liam right behind me.

"There's no sense in arguing, because you're going to lose. Just like you lost that bet."

He closes the door behind us, and his hand is on the small of my back as he walks me to the elevator.

"I didn't lose the bet." I'm not giving Liam Moretti the satisfaction.

"You did, and you owe me a date."

My nose twitches, and I slam the elevator button abruptly for down.

"Someone's cranky. Not enough sleep?" Liam jokes, like he's talking about that little kid at his house, not a grown-ass woman.

I elbow him to shut up, and he takes a step back, giving me some distance.

Finally!

The elevator dings and opens on the sixth floor. I step inside, and Liam is right next to me. "You can relax; I don't make it a habit of fainting in elevators."

He raises an eyebrow. "Are you sure?"

I punch the button for the first floor and ignore him.

It's hard to do when he steps closer to me.

I glare at him.

"I'm just trying to be helpful!" He throws his arms up in the air, but he's practically right beside me, invading my personal space.

"You and helpful aren't two words that belong in the same sentence."

He mocks injury like I've wounded his chest and throws a hand against his heart. "That burns, Firebreather."

"I guess you gave me the right nickname."

The elevator doors open, and I hurry out before he has time to reply. I'm jetting out the foyer and through the double doors like I'm on a mission. And I am, to get home and away from Liam.

I grumble under my breath, pissed at myself that I'm not clever enough to come up with a nickname for him.

Knowing my luck, I'll think up one when he's gone.

Liam is right behind me as I hurry across the lawn, intending to take a short cut, a few steps less, toward my building.

"In a hurry?" Liam guesses, and he's got long legs, so it just takes him a few strides to keep up.

I feel like I'm running, which isn't doing my racing heart any favors. The heat is also beating the hell out of me as it starts to finally lower along the horizon.

It's not humid like Florida, but the heat and sunlight are enough to make me uncomfortable.

I've never quite understood it, but heat and I don't get along. Winter is fine. I despise the cold, but it doesn't make me sick.

Heat is an entirely different beast. I've spent more time in and out of doctor's offices and the emergency room, getting IVs for dehydration. I faint more in the heat. I also can't seem to focus, like my brain is a million miles away. It's as if I step out into the sun and I'm instantly sucked of my life. I prefer the night and no, I'm not a vampire. Although at times it does feel a bit that way.

The heat is sweltering, and I grab the door handle, yanking it open, grateful for the cool blast of air inside as the air conditioning is pouring in and making the place bearable.

My head spins, dizziness overwhelming all of my senses.

I should have consumed a second drink of water in Sophia's room. I finished the first bottle, not that it seems to have mattered.

I focus on putting one foot in front of the other.

I am not going to pass out in front of Liam Moretti.

Not like I haven't already done that once today, but twice, absolutely not!

I will myself to stay upright, the cold air helping bring my senses back, one by one.

I'm in front of the elevator, staring at the button, and Liam steps beside me and pushes it.

"What floor?" Liam asks before we so much as step into the elevator.

He must notice the glazed look on my face, the fact that I can't seem to focus and even so much as talking takes far too much energy.

Tunnel vision.

It sucks.

"Six," I manage to rasp. I want to remark that he should remember he came up to my room, we kissed, but the words are too heavy on my tongue. They take more strength than I can muster.

I step forward, the nausea rearing its ugly head, sweeping over me as I grip the handrail in the elevator.

Not fucking, again.

Please.

The elevator isn't nearly as cool as the first floor, and I feel the telltale signs of trouble brewing.

Please, no.

Sweat licks my forehead, beading down my skin. My

vision flickers for a moment as I sway, and Liam's arm is right there on my hip.

"I've got you," he whispers into my ear, his breath causing me to shudder.

I'm not expecting his touch, his breath, the heat of his body, which makes my heart race even faster.

I don't notice Liam pressing the button for the sixth floor.

I can't say I see much of anything as dark spots pepper my vision.

Fuck me.

My legs go weak and my breathing intensifies, quickens, as though I'm chasing after the last light in my eyes.

His arms are around me, and he scoops me up into his arms before I have time to process what he's doing. The sweeping darkness tries to take over, but I'm hauled against his chest as the elevator door dings and we reach our destination.

At least that's where I think we are, because my eyes are shut and I'm resting my head on his chest.

I don't even care about the embarrassment and humiliation that I know I will face come tomorrow.

He carries me out of the elevator, and the blast of cold air in the hallway is a welcome relief to the heat and nausea rolling over me like waves.

"Where's your key, babe? I'm going to need to let you into your room."

"In my pocket."

"I'm going to have to put you down." Liam carries me up to my dorm room. He may not have remembered the floor, but he remembered which door is mine.

"I don't—"

He gently sets me down on the ground in a seated position, my back against the wall, and he bends down to my level. He keeps one hand on me at all times, making sure I don't fall over. "Do you want to grab those keys, or should I?"

Since when is Liam a gentleman?

My hands tremble along with my body as I reach into my pocket and retrieve my key. I hand him the keychain, and he raises an eyebrow as he reads the inscription of the tarot card design, but he doesn't say a word.

Not enough sage for this shit.

Describes my life perfectly, especially today.

He keeps one hand on me while unlocking the door and pushing it open. Then, he bends down and scoops me into his arms, carrying me to my bed.

"Don't argue with me, Firebreather, but there is zero chance I'm leaving you alone. I'm staying the night."

FOURTEEN

LIAM

"You don't have to stay over," Bristol tells me, yet again. She's stretched out on her mattress, and I'm seated on the desk chair, pulled up alongside her bed.

Me leaving is the absolute worst idea.

"Well, I'm not leaving you alone. You don't have a roommate. Is there anyone else I can call for you?"

"I'm fine. I just need to sleep it off." She closes her eyes and feigns sleep.

"Like a hangover?" I'm skeptical. She's fainted more

than once today. I'd be an asshole if I left her all alone.

My instinct tells me to take her to the emergency room.

Her silence irritates me, and I scoot closer, the chair squeaking against the linoleum flooring, forcing her to open an eye as she glares at me.

"I'm trying to sleep, Moretti."

All the lights are still on in her dorm room. I don't think she's actually trying to sleep, it's more of her way to shut me up.

I'm learning to speak *Bristol Greyson* a little too well.

Pursing my lips, I have an idea.

She's going to hate me for it, but well, she already hates me.

"Remember that bet?"

Bristol grumbles under her breath.

"I don't think I'm up for going out, Liam." Her nostrils flare, and she gives me the side-eye.

Oh yeah, she's definitely going to hate me even more.

Good.

“I’m calling it.”

“What?” her brow twitches, and she rolls onto her side, keeping her legs outstretched. “What are you yammering on about?”

“I’m going to take you out on that date tonight.”

She snorts. “Do I really look capable of going out tonight, Liam? Read the fucking room.”

A smirk falls on my lips. “Oh, I am. You’re accompanying me where I want to go.”

“Fuck off.” She throws up her hand, giving me the finger. I imagine it takes her a lot of energy, based solely on the expression she’s wearing.

I lean closer, getting in her face, riling her up. “I love your energy.”

“You’re a real piece of trash, Liam. Forcing me to go out with you when I’m sick.”

I glance at my phone, checking the temperature this evening, to make sure it’s not too chilly and if she’ll need a light coat before going out.

"Hate-date," I say with a smirk. "Let's call it what it is."

She snips at me, "At least you have one thing right. The only thing we'll ever agree on."

I pull up the maps app on my phone and type in the location of where I want us to go. I keep it out of her sight. There's zero chance she'd agree with my decision.

I shove my phone back into my pocket. I retrieve her keys and lift Bristol into my arms.

"Are you planning on carrying me on our date?" Her arms wrap around my neck, but it's only for support. "I hate you," she grumbles into my ear.

"I'm sure you'll hate me even more after."

"Why? Do you plan on forcing yourself on me?"

I bite down on my bottom lip.

Her remark stings, but I choose to ignore it.

I carry her out of her dorm room, and thankfully, the door locks automatically behind us. I bring her down to the elevator, and she rests her head on my chest. I hit the button to go down.

For a moment, I can't tell if she's falling asleep or passing out.

Until she opens her mouth, and the silence vanishes. "You can put me down. I'm capable of walking."

I'm not sure that she is—without passing out.

"Only if you'll let me keep an arm around you." I don't want to risk her fainting and hitting her head.

"Fine," she snarls at me, and I carefully place her feet on the ground in front of the elevator.

The doors open, and she steps inside, swaying slightly, but my hand is around her waist, keeping her upright.

I press the button for the main floor and feel her back up, pressing her body against mine.

My arms encircle her waist, and for a moment, if I forget all the shit from today, this might actually feel nice. Like a couple.

But Bristol and I aren't anything but complicated not-friends. I'm not sure if we still qualify as enemies. After tonight, we might once again.

I'll take my chances.

The elevator doors open, and I walk out with her, accompanying her to my vehicle. She sways a bit, unsteady on her feet, but I'm right there, my arm against her waist, holding her to me.

Once we're both situated in the car, I use the maps app to get us to the destination, because I'm not that familiar with the area.

Ten minutes later, I'm pulling up out front of Great Falls Emergency Room.

Bristol lets out a huff.

"You fucking didn't. You want to go here. On our date?" She points at the entrance as I pull up at the front and park the car long enough to grab a wheelchair.

"I want you to feel better."

"The ER can't do anything for me, Liam. This is a colossal waste of time."

"Such a big word," I taunt her, doing my best to distract her. "You owe me one date. This is my date."

"You're fucking weird." Bristol shakes her head but doesn't tell me no.

"If the situation were reversed, and I was the one fainting, would you want me to go into the ER to get checked out?"

Her eyes glint with anger. "I'd kick you out of my car and let you die on the side of the road."

"I don't believe you." I help her into a wheelchair and then stroll her inside past the front entrance. "Don't go anywhere."

"Where the hell am I going to run off to?" I hear her shouting back at me.

I run back to the car to park it in the lot nearby and jog back inside.

By the time I'm inside, merely two minutes later at most, Harper has a clipboard with a stack of papers to fill out. She shoves them at me.

"The paperwork is yours, *sweetheart*."

"Sarcasm looks good on you," I say with a smile. I glance down at the blank pages. She's filled nothing out.

Okay, this should be interesting.

I know her first and last name.

"Date of birth?" I ask.

She gives me the information along with her legal address.

"I also need your insurance information."

Bristol digs into her pocket for her phone and shoves it at me.

"It's under the case."

I unclasp the case, and behind it are her insurance card and her identification.

"Bristol," the triage nurse calls her first name, and I push her in the wheelchair into the small room.

"You can fill out the rest of the forms out there," the triage nurse informs me while ushering me out of the room and closing the door behind them.

I take a seat, copying the insurance information over and putting my name down as one of her emergency contacts.

I stare at the box beneath my name. *Relationship to patient.*

Boyfriend won't suffice. They'll never let me back if I don't put I'm a blood relative. Husband? We're not wearing wedding bands, and she barely looks eighteen.

I opt for brother, which may or may not end well for me.

This whole night is a disaster in the making.

Besides, Bristol already hates me, which at least makes a sibling relationship believable in this place.

I fill out as much as I can and wait for Bristol, in case she has any allergies or other medical information to include on the forms. I certainly don't know the date of her last period or all of her current symptoms.

I marked the obvious one: fainting.

Waiting for Bristol, I play with her phone, trying her month and date to unlock her device.

Bingo.

That was way too easy.

She'll end me if she realizes I have access to her phone. I scroll through her contacts and land on *Dad*.

I know she's close with her parents, at least I've seen her at games with her father recently.

Yes, she asked me not to contact anyone, but that was before we went to the emergency room. Besides, won't he see the bill? Isn't it better for him to know what's going on with his daughter?

I send myself his contact information before messaging him from my phone.

Liam: Hi, I'm friends with your daughter, Bristol. She fainted this afternoon on campus. I drove her to the ER. I'll stay with her and keep you updated.

Within seconds, my phone rings.

"Hello?"

"Is Bristol okay?" Kyler's voice is filled with concern. I recognize it from the press conferences I've seen of him on television.

I've always imagined what it'd be like to talk to an NHL player. I never thought it'd be over the phone, discussing his daughter's health.

"She's with the triage nurse right now." Guilt ebbs at me. Maybe I shouldn't have worried her father, at least until after we knew what was going on.

"I'm glad you called. She will probably need I.V. fluids. In the past, that seems to have helped."

The door to the triage nurse's office opens. "Bristol is coming back, I should go."

"Yes, please text and keep me updated," Kyler says.

I stand, helping wheel Bristol back to the waiting area with me. "Who were you on the phone with?" Bristol asks.

I ignore her question and bring her to sit in front of my chair. "You might want to fill out the last of these questions." I hand her the clipboard and pen.

"Brother?" She glances up at me, glaring, and inhales sharply. "What kind of brother takes his sister on a date to the emergency room?"

Thankfully, the emergency room is empty, or there might be some questionable eyes shooting my way right now.

"The kind who cares about her?" My voice raises an octave. "I can wait here when you go back."

Bristol shakes her head and winces. "No. If I'm going to be dragged back there, you're coming with me."

She glances down at the forms, jots the information necessary and shoves it back at me to hold on to.

"Worst date ever," she mutters under her breath.

"The worst date would be if *I'm* the reason that you're in the ER."

"You *are* the reason I'm here!"

Exhaling, I stare at her, not the least afraid of Bristol. I don't back down, not with her, not ever. "That's not fair." I pin her with my stare, and she finally glances away. "I only suggested this to help you. Do you think this is what I wanted for our first date?"

"We're not going on a date, Liam." She folds her arms across her chest.

"And why not?" I ask, pushing her for an answer. I half-expect her to tell me that this is the date and I have to suck it up.

"You hate me for starters. Why would you want to date someone you hate?" She raises an eyebrow, waiting for my answer.

"I don't hate you—"

Bristol doesn't look the least bit convinced, and I'm not about to pour my feelings out to her. Honestly, I'm not entirely sure what I feel for her. The girl knows how to leave a man conflicted.

"Well, I hate you. You stress me out. You make everything a million times worse because—"

Her words sting, but I don't so much as flinch. "Because what?" I ask, waiting for her to elaborate.

"Because you're ... you!"

FIFTEEN

LUCA

Dante surprisingly gave me quite a bit of time off on the weekends after the mishap where I got my ass kicked.

In fact, I've had the entire summer when I'm not being forced to do as he commands.

We've agreed to have dinner with them twice a month while I'm recovering.

Thankfully, dinner was last weekend, which gave me this weekend to focus entirely on Harper and Zeke.

I love having summers off, not worrying about attending classes and studying for exams. It's given

Harper and me more time to find our footing in our new marriage.

It's been good, better than I thought it would be, after all the drama we've endured the past few months.

Harper is sound asleep after yesterday's festivities in the bedroom, which were spicier than even I imagined. Finding out your wife likes to roleplay and then making your fantasy come true, holy hell.

She makes one sexy little nurse.

I'm the luckiest man alive!

Zeke runs around the living room while I'm in the kitchen, cooking breakfast.

"Daddy, I eat bacon."

"Yes, you can have some when it cools off." I don't want him to eat anything too hot and get burned. The guy has crocodile tears that make even me want to cry.

I'd do anything to protect Zeke—and that extends to Harper as well.

Protecting them isn't easy.

Massimo DeLuca is a constant fear rattling through my head.

For a while, I was uncertain if he was still alive.

Turns out he is, and I want him dead.

But he's been dark, their network quiet since the last encounter with Harper at the grocery store and park.

Dante believes we damaged their operation enough to slow it down. They're still trafficking girls, but not out of our city.

But give it time.

They'll return with a vengeance and a vendetta against me.

I have to take Massimo's threats seriously. We have cameras outside the property, and the feed is transmitted to Dante's men, who can watch over the house 24/7 and ensure that everyone is safe, especially my family.

But surveillance isn't enough, and Dante's men aren't nearby. They're an hour plus away. Which leaves Liam, Ashton, and me to handle any situation that may arise.

Dante's given us weapons and ammo, which we keep locked away and out of Zeke's reach. I hope never to use any of it in my home, but it's a concern that weighs heavily on me.

It's not something I talk to Harper about. She has her own worries. She doesn't need to know about Massimo's threat.

It would only worry and upset her, which is the last thing I want to do.

"Daddy, bacon!" Zeke stomps his feet, demanding that I pay attention to him.

I pull three slices of bacon from the pan and place them on a plate with a paper towel, trying to dry off the grease.

"Daddy!" Zeke doesn't seem to have much patience. I really wish that were something Harper could teach him, because I'm not exactly a patient man, either.

"I know, Zeke, you just have to wait until it cools down."

"I'm starving. I'm going to die!" Zeke exclaims.

The kid is all about theatrics.

I try not to roll my eyes. "You aren't going to die. How about you go nicely wake up your mom, and breakfast will be ready when you both get back?"

Zeke tears out of the kitchen, nearly tripping over his little feet. He runs into the bedroom and I can imagine Harper trying to pull him under the covers for a little more shuteye.

"Mommy, no sleep! Bacon," I hear his little voice over the stove with its sizzle from the bacon, and I kick the stove fan on to keep the house from getting too smoky.

The front door creaks open, and I glance at Liam, who is doing the walk of shame, except the man has no shame.

He is, however, wearing yesterday's clothes.

"Finally decided to come home." I can't help but smirk at him, but he's wearing a grave expression on his face.

"What is it?"

Liam sighs heavily, running a hand through his hair. "Whoever is threatening Harper, it's not over. I caught some guy snooping outside the house."

"You what?" I step away from the stove and head for the door.

"It's already taken care of. I left him with a black eye, and he'll need to ice his family jewels." Liam snickers. "I did manage to grab his wallet, memorize his address, and threaten that if he ever shows his face on campus, I'll kill him and his family."

"So, who is he?" It has to be someone on Massimo's crew.

"Roberto Gianni. When I say I memorized his address, I took a photo of it. I'll send it to you."

"Please, do that." I exhale heavily and head back to the stove.

"Was he carrying any weapons on him?"

I need as much information as I can get from Liam. His father is mafia, it's not like he's foreign to this sort of thing.

"He had a gun on him. I disarmed him before I made him hit the road."

"He could come back." I glance at Liam. The doors are locked, but I'm not convinced we're safe here.

"If he does, it'll be with a crew. The guy was barely capable of landing a swing to this pretty face." Liam points at his jawline. "Don't get me wrong, I'm fast in a fight, but the guy seemed more like reconnaissance than anything else. He wasn't expecting to get caught. Next time, we'll be ready." Liam folds his arms across his chest.

I don't like knowing that Massimo's men are coming after my family. "Next time?" I don't want there to be a next time. I went them all dead.

"I'm not worried," Liam mumbles. Yawning, he rubs his eyes. "You shouldn't be either."

How can I not be concerned? This isn't the first incident, and it's clearly not a coincidence if they're showing up on campus and at our house.

"They're coming after my family," I grunt. "I can't just ignore this mess. They need to be stopped."

"We'll keep an eye on Harper and Zeke, like we've been doing. They'll be safe." Liam's words do little to reassure me.

I should call Dante, keep him informed.

But things will inevitably get more heated when I do reach out to him.

What other choice do I have?

There's no winning this war, not without getting my hands dirty.

I focus on the bacon, making sure it doesn't burn as I flip the next batch on the stove.

It's not Liam's problem to worry about, he doesn't even work for Dante.

I glance up from the stove at Liam. "Didn't get much sleep last night?" It's an easy guess, seeing as how he's rolling in at this hour in yesterday's clothes.

"Spent the night in the emergency room."

"Is everything okay?" He doesn't look sick or injured, but for all I know, some girl could have broken his dick.

"Yeah, I'm fine. I went there in support of a ... friend." He grimaces on the last word.

Weird.

I ignore it.

"Okay, well, I'm making bacon, and I'm going to put some eggs on in a few minutes. You're welcome to join us, there will be plenty of food."

"I think I'm going to climb into bed and take a nap. Is it all right if I catch up with you later?"

"By all means. Hopefully, we don't keep you up."

The bedroom door from down the hallway squeaks open, but it's not coming from Liam's room, which I can see from the kitchen.

Ashton and Nova are awake.

Can't say I'm thrilled that they're sharing the same room. I'm not an idiot. I'm well aware that they're sleeping together, but still, it's a little uncomfortable for me.

Pretty much everyone in the house other than Zeke has told me to get over it.

They're happy.

I should be happy for both of them.

I'm really trying to be happy for them.

I'm no longer angry with Ashton for hiding the fact that he was dating my little sister. That anger dissipated the moment he saved my life back in the spring.

He could have left me to die in that basement.

Maybe he should have, because I'd been an ass to him, repeatedly.

Instead, he saved my life.

Thankfully, he'd brought a gun to the surveillance mission. Ashton was better prepared than I was.

"Morning," Ashton says, and his arm is around Nova's hip. He presses a kiss to her lips before she sneaks off into the bathroom, alone.

I'm assuming the "morning" comment was to me, but with those two, you never know. "Good morning. I've got bacon cooking, and I was going to put on some eggs after. Do you want to start on the eggs?"

Zeke comes running out of my bedroom with Harper right behind him.

"Eww, no eggs, Daddy." Zeke overhears us and comes barreling into the kitchen. "Pancakes, please."

Sighing, I wasn't planning on making any pancakes, but it's hard to say no to Zeke. I know he's not keen on eggs, but I've been trying to make them different ways. I'm confident he'll eventually like them. I've just got to figure out what way to make them for him.

Harper comes into the kitchen, the space tight with three adults plus Zeke. "I'll make him pancakes. We have some in the freezer I can heat up."

Zeke claps and then climbs into his booster seat at the table. The food isn't quite ready yet, but he's got quite an appetite. He's also grown a lot over the past few months. I can't believe how much he's changed. He's gone from baby to little boy so fast.

My phone buzzes in my pocket, and I grab it, glancing at the screen and grumbling under my breath.

It's Dante.

He probably saw the surveillance footage outside the house. If Liam knocked around one of Massimo's men on the property, then it's on camera.

I answer the phone with one hand, and with the other, I'm diligently working on cooking bacon.

"Busy morning." Dante doesn't even offer a hello.

I exhale and nod, forgetting for a moment he can't see me.

"Yeah, we had an unexpected visitor."

"I noticed." Dante's voice is tense. "Luca, I need you and Ashton to return to the house this afternoon."

I bite down on my tongue. I knew he would call us again and want us to return to working for him, I was just hoping he'd push it back a little longer. Like next semester, or maybe the following one.

But the appearance of Roberto Gianni showing up also tells me that trouble is brewing, and I don't like trouble showing up at my front door.

"What time?" I glance at Ashton and mouth "Dante" to him.

"The sooner, the better. I need to get you caught up to speed on Massimo. He's been spotted in town, and we think we have the location of his next shipment."

Exhaling a sigh, I don't exactly have another choice.

I despise the work my father does, but Massimo is far worse. The things he's doing to those women and possibly children, it burns me up inside.

"We'll be there," I grunt before ending the call. I need to tell him what happened with Harper. I've been delaying the inevitable, trying to deal with it ourselves.

"What's going on?" Harper asks, catching the tail end of the conversation.

"Dante called. He wants Ashton and me back at the house this afternoon. As soon as possible."

She purses her lips together, her mind reeling. "It sounded urgent. Everything okay?"

I don't dare tell her about Massimo and the work that we suspect he's involved in. She saw the bruises, but I never told her the specifics.

There was no reason to worry her.

The less she knows, the better.

"Dante has something he needs us to help him with."

Leaving her is wrong. There's a lead ball in the pit of my stomach, making me anxious and nauseous, and the pain in my chest returns. Except it's not from the broken ribs or bruises, it's worry.

With the threats and now two men having shown up on campus, I can't take any chances with my wife or son. Especially when Ashton and I won't be here to protect her.

"Pack a bag for us and Zeke. You're coming with us." It's not a question.

She stares at me, and I try to alleviate some of her concern. "Mom would love to help with Zeke, and we'll all be home in a couple of days."

Harper watches me, like she senses something is off. Probably from the sweat on my forehead and my voice not quite its usual tone.

"A couple of days with your family," Harper repeats.

She's clearly thinking it over, but if she says no, I'll have to find another way to convince her, because her staying here without me isn't an option.

"It's Sunday. I thought you only worked with him on the weekends." Harper's brow is pinched, and she rubs at her forehead. She's on the verge of something, like she's trying to piece it all together, but I don't think whatever she's thinking is anything close to the truth.

“It’s also summer,” I remind her. “He’s given me the past several months off—”

“Because you were nearly beaten to death.” Her hands are on my arm, pulling me toward her. “What’s going on, Luca?”

“Babe, I’ve got to finish cooking on the stove.” I force a smile, but when that isn’t enough, I hand Ashton the fork to pull the bacon off the pan when it’s ready.

I wrap my arms around Harper, pulling her tight against me. “Everything’s going to be fine.”

“You don’t know that,” she whispers, staring up at me, worry etched all over her beautiful face. “Your parents scare me, and then that incident at the store—"

I lean in, brushing my lips hungrily against hers, taking a taste, trying to convince her that I’m here and I’m not going anywhere. “Come with me.”

Her fingers tangle in my hair at the nape of my neck, and I deepen the kiss, pulling her tighter, harder, craving her touch.

“You two, get a room.” Nova’s voice startles me.

"Dante called us back for work," Ashton says, glancing at Nova.

Her bottom lip juts out in a pout. "That's a bummer. I wanted us to go out on a date tonight."

"Promise I'll make it up to you," Ashton says, blowing Nova a kiss. She stalks around, stealing a kiss from him while he's cooking on the stove. "We can always have our little late-night video chats."

I wince, listening to my best friend flirt with my little sister.

I drop several chaste kisses on Harper's nose and cheeks. "What do you say about spending the weekend at my parents' house?"

Harper grimaces, her eyes flickering. "Are you sure that's a good idea? I mean, Zeke can be a handful, and I'm not sure your parents actually like me. They're civil and polite to me, but like me—that's a stretch."

"They don't dislike you, they're just ... different."

"They're mafia."

It's not something that she needs to remind me of; I'm well aware who my father is. In fact, it's the reason I want her under their roof. If I can't watch over her to ensure her safety, then Dante and his men can.

"Yes," I whisper and lean closer, teasing her with my lips.

I can sense her hesitation, feel her tense against me.

My fingers tangle in her hair, guiding her lips back down to mine. My movements are rough but deliberate, taking control, showing her what she'll be getting or missing.

Seeing as how it seems she needs a bit of convincing for tonight.

Her lips part, hungry for more as I hover but don't kiss her. Her breath is warm, and it caresses my cheek. Her eyelids are heavy, and she leans in to steal another taste, but I pull back, teasing her. "We don't have time now," I whisper cheekily, "but tonight—"

Harper moans, and I swear that delicious sound goes straight to my cock.

Fuck me.

I playfully bite down on her bottom lip, tugging it between my teeth.

This time, she whimpers, and my heart speeds up, my body desiring to explore every inch of her. If I don't slow down this minute, it's going to be a very uncomfortable ride in the car.

"Come with me."

She blinks a few times and grins. "You know that's my favorite part."

I laugh, leaning my forehead against hers, as if we're the only ones in the room.

I can hear Nova's footsteps hurrying away now that she's heard far too much.

"Come with me to my parents'."

Harper's nose scrunches at the words and pouts. "I just want to come with you." That sexy tone stirs my insides and makes my cock twitch.

I drop a kiss to her lips, reluctantly pulling farther back. Another minute of *that* type of talk, and I'll be throwing her over my shoulder and carrying her to the bedroom, caveman style.

I lean my back against the counter, letting it offer me support because Harper makes my head spin.

"Pack a bag."

She rolls her lips together and then finally nods. "I'll grab stuff for Zeke as well. Nova, are you joining us?"

"Yeah, let me go pack my things. Give me ten minutes?" Nova hurries down the hallway.

"That's fine. We still need to finish breakfast, clean up, and get Zeke dressed for the day." I breathe a heavy sigh when Harper heads out of the kitchen and has agreed to join us this weekend.

Ashton turns around to face me. "Everything okay? You really pushed the idea of Harper joining us today. That's a little ... unusual for you."

"Liam came home this morning. Caught someone outside our place."

"Shit." Ashton frowns. "It seemed too quiet around here after the last threat..." he trails off, glancing in the direction of the hallway where the girls ran off. "Do we know anything about the guy who showed up?"

"Liam snapped a photo of his identification. He's supposed to text me a copy. I'll make sure that we get the text before we leave."

Ashton hands me back the fork. "Here, get help with the bacon so we can get out of here. I'm almost done with the eggs."

Nova and Harper both pack overnight bags, but I swear the girls packed enough for a week's trip.

I don't argue about the unnecessary extras they're bringing along. There's plenty of trunk space for the bags.

Ashton and I toss everything in the trunk. The girls and Zeke squeeze into the backseat while I drive and Ashton sits up front with me.

There is lots of chatter the entire drive up to the compound. Nova makes us swear not to tell anyone at home she's dating Ashton.

I share a quiet glance with Ashton because Dante knows. And I'm pretty sure Moreno knows.

"Don't worry," Harper says. "I'm pretty sure that's a conversation that's not going to randomly come up."

"I know, but it always worries me. Like if Dad comes knocking on my bedroom door and Ashton is in my room," Nova says.

"Then sleep in my room." Ashton glances over his shoulder at Nova. He extends an arm, reaching for her, like the two of them can't quite get enough of each other.

Sounds familiar.

"Can you guys not sleep in Ashton's room? Last time you did that, I could hear you. Not even noise-canceling headphones could drown the two of you out." It's a memory that I don't want to remember, barging in on the two of them in bed together.

"Oh, like we don't hear the two of you all the frickin' time." Ashton lets go of Nova's hand and glares at me. "I'm glad you two are finally getting along, but some of us like to sleep in."

I catch a glimpse of Harper in my rearview mirror as she laughs. Her eyes are bright, and her cheeks are red. Oh, she's definitely embarrassed. I like that look on her, how her skin is flushed, and it reminds me of another time she gets those colorful cheeks.

"We're not that loud." I glower at Ashton. "You're just stirring shit up."

"Language!" Harper scolds me.

"Sorry." I grimace. I've been trying to do better, watch myself around Zeke.

Hopefully, he's not paying attention and didn't hear my curse word.

As we pull up out front, storm clouds are brewing in the distance. It's going to make for a long night if it's thundering and we're stuck doing surveillance on Massimo in the rain.

I try not to let it ruin my day. We head out of the car, Ashton and I grabbing everyone's bags while Harper unbuckles Zeke and carries him to the front door, right behind Nova.

"We're home!" Nova shouts as she heads inside, announcing us.

It's not like security doesn't get the first inkling of our arrival when we have to punch in the code at the gate. Sometimes they have a man standing guard outside at the guard post, it depends on how busy things are with Dante or the current level of security he feels is necessary.

I slip out of my shoes as I enter the house last. "I'm going to take our bags upstairs." I glance at Harper, making sure she heard me before I head upstairs.

"Okay, thanks." Harper looks a bit nervous. It's not like this is the first time she's stayed at my parents' house, but it's been a while since she's spent the night. As long as she doesn't go snooping, things will be fine.

I'm actually feeling a bit relieved knowing that Harper and Zeke are here. I won't have to worry about them while I'm away, and I can remain focused on Massimo.

I'd love to be wrong about him, that Massimo wasn't trafficking women, just selling counterfeit merchandise, but I doubt he's in the business of selling lingerie. It doesn't fit him as a mafia boss.

Two dons, one city.

Nothing good will come of the war brewing between the two organizations. My loyalty and allegiance is to my wife, first and foremost. I'd do anything to protect her and my son. Dante falls in line far behind them, but I know my place, my job, and my responsibilities.

I never thought I'd choose Dante over anyone else, but having met Massimo, who happens to be my uncle, talk about mind-blowing, I want nothing to do with him.

Dante is a monster.

Massimo is the devil.

And what does that make me, the man who does Dante's bidding?

I place Zeke's smaller bag on the dresser in his bedroom and then our shared bag on the dresser in our bedroom. I like knowing that I get to sleep in here with Harper.

It at least makes the thought of going to bed tonight not awful.

I've had trouble falling asleep under Dante's roof for years. Working for him hasn't made it any easier, and each day that I'm here, I only grow more tired.

I can't make mistakes, it could get Ashton or myself killed.

Closing the door behind me, I head downstairs, hearing chatter through the halls. It's unusual to have the house so lively, except when shit is going down.

But today's chatter is upbeat, friendly, boisterous. I'm not used to witnessing it in this home.

Stepping into the hallway, I walk toward the laughter and pleasant sounds as I catch sight of Zeke showing off his dancing moves and Ashton is playing some ridiculous music with his phone to cheer the kid on.

Even Harper is dancing along with Zeke, and as I watch from the doorjamb, I realize they're doing the same dance moves.

A smile spreads across my face, watching her with Zeke; it makes me want to put a baby in her.

I refrain from striding across the space and capturing her lips with mine. I want to badly, but I also don't want to stop watching because the way she's swaying her hips will give me a few new fantasies for the two of us to try out—stripper and dancer.

Yes, I'm a guy, which makes my mind constantly

thinking about Harper and sex. It's two of my favorite things, the third being Zeke.

The song ends and everyone, including me, begins clapping for them.

Zeke grins and claps proudly as well, taking a bow.

The kid is a real showman.

"There you are," Harper says, reaching for my hand, pulling me into the room with them.

I grab a seat on the couch, yanking her onto my lap. I can't ever get enough of the woman who has stolen my heart.

And then there's Zeke, who has grown so fast and will soon be three. He loves dragons and pretty much any animal that roars.

"Luca," Dante's voice bellows over the room as he stands in the doorframe. He gestures for me to get up and come with him. "I'd like to see you as well, Ashton."

"Business calls," I whisper to Harper, pressing a soft kiss to her lips.

"Be safe." She stares at me, the worry lines wrinkling her forehead. I kiss them away, as if that will absolve away her concerns.

I wish it would ease my own fears. I'm not afraid to face Massimo. I'm worried about my family.

"You know I will." I steal one more kiss before following Dante down the hallway and pause as he leads us toward the basement.

SIXTEEN

LUCA

When my father escorts Ashton and me down into the basement, I'm expecting a prisoner. Secretly, I'm hoping it's Massimo.

The compound is a fortress, but the jail downstairs is probably my father's most prized possession. He prides himself on keeping men just long enough to have his interrogator work their magic.

Then they're removed from the property.

I've never quite known what that entails.

Obviously, they're dead, but does he incinerate

them, bury them, drown their bodies in the lake, or something else far more sinister?

I've spent many wakeless nights under Dante's roof wondering all the ways they erase a man from existence and never seem to get caught.

I suppose I'll be entrusted with such secrets if my father truly wants me to run his empire.

"Why bring us down here?" Ashton is right behind me. He's the first with questions, showing his interest.

I'm more curious about how we intend to stop the men threatening my family and where do I find them.

"I wanted someplace we could talk, plan, speak freely." He leads us past the prison cells, and there's a door in the back, leading to a room with maps on the walls, a large wooden table in the center. He's got a map spread across the table.

His men are already down here, talking, waiting for us.

I've never been this far back in the basement. The

door isn't a surprise, but the room behind it, I never knew what lay inside.

Dante steps into the room and Halsey, the capo, one of Dante's support teams, steps aside, giving him space at the center.

Halsey has his own team of men who do his bidding, a hierarchy of sorts, leading all the way up to my father.

The room grows quiet when Dante approaches. Bruno, Alessandro, Nico, and Zeno stand around the table.

Ashton and I stand at the opposite end, beside Moreno.

"Catch us all up to speed, Halsey." Dante stares at his capo, letting him give the mission assignment since he's leading the team.

"Massimo will be making a delivery this afternoon." Halsey points at the map of Breckenridge. It's a zoomed-in version of the location, but it's not the same road or cabin where Ashton and I had run into trouble.

I suck in a sharp breath.

Just knowing that I could lay eyes on Massimo, brings my anger simmering to the surface.

"What's the delivery, exactly?" I need to know that I'm not wrong and he's trafficking women.

"Go take a look for yourself," Dante says, pointing to the boxes in the corner of the room, stacked against the wall.

There are two large boxes about knee-high, stacked upon one another.

Ashton remains at the table while I approach the boxes. I open the lid and peer inside at the women's lingerie, sex toys, and boxes of condoms thrown together haphazardly. "They're trafficking women?"

"Kidnapping women," Dante says, "and then holding them hostage, forcing them to—well, you get the picture."

I'd suspected it all along, and the thought sickens me no less today than it did months ago.

I wanted to be wrong.

My stomach roils with disgust.

"They threatened my family, my wife and son." Anger roars through my blood. I shove the box to the ground, the contents tipping over, spilling onto the floor.

Dante nods. "We managed to steal their supplies, but it won't slow down their operation, but I need a team to take out Massimo and his crew."

I bend down, catching sight of something that doesn't quite fit the contents of the box. In the bottom is a stuffed dragon. It's the same one Zeke has on his bed. Except this one has a dagger right through its head.

SEVENTEEN

HARPER

Luca and Ashton have been gone for a couple of hours. Nova has been spending the afternoon entertaining Zeke and chatting with me in the playroom.

Zeke keeps showing us all the new toys that he's discovered. Most of them look well-loved; I'm relieved Nikki isn't going out buying dozens of new toys every time we come to visit.

"Do you mind keeping an eye on him for a few minutes?" I smile at Nova as she glances at her phone.

"Sure. Bathroom break?"

"How'd you guess?" The smile feels forced, but hopefully, she doesn't notice since she's a bit enthralled with her phone. Is she texting Ashton?

I give Zeke a quick kiss on the cheek. "Be good for Aunty Nova."

He ignores me, pushing me aside for the train set that has stolen all of his attention.

I hurry out of the playroom and down the hallway, searching for Dante. I breeze past the bathroom when Moreno makes eye contact with me as he approaches from the far end of the hallway.

"Looking for the restroom?" Moreno raises an eyebrow.

It's no surprise that he won't tolerate snooping.

"Actually, I wanted to speak with Dante. Can you show me to him?"

"He's busy at the moment." Moreno sighs and gestures to the playroom. "You should go and keep your son company. This place isn't for you to run around in like a child."

My gaze narrows as I glance him over. “I wasn’t running.” I clear my throat, stepping closer. Moreno hovers above me, but he doesn’t scare me nearly as much as his boss. Moreno doesn’t have the same authority. I ball my hands into fists, my teeth clench, and I growl up at him, “Take me to Dante.”

“Your funeral,” he mutters and leads me down the hallway to a closed door, the window made of frosted glass. “His office.”

Moreno knocks against the glass door.

“Come inside.” Dante’s rough voice sends a shiver down my spine.

I can’t back down. I need answers.

Moreno opens the door for me. “Harper would like a word with you.” They exchange a silent glance between one another. “I warned her that you were busy.”

“I am, but I will make time for my daughter-in-law. Come in.” Dante gestures me inside, and I step foot inside his office, the door closing abruptly behind me.

The room is far cooler than I expected with the heat blasting the house.

Perhaps he likes it chillier, or maybe his heart truly is made of ice and freezes over his office.

"Have a seat." He points to the chair across from his desk, the leather vacant, waiting for me.

Slowly, I approach his desk and then take a seat. Sitting at the edge of the chair, my hands fiddling in my lap, I meet his heavy stare.

"What can I do for you, Harper?" Dante's gaze tightens.

"I need to know what's going on with Luca. The bruises on his chest, the broken ribs. Whatever you're sending him into—an ambush, or whatever it is—you need to keep him safe."

He doesn't smile.

He stares right through me, giving no hint of emotion at all.

Silence fills the space between us, and then there's a slight boom when the heat kicks on, and I nearly jump out of my seat.

That seems to amuse him.

A crooked smile reaches his face. “What has my son told you?”

“Absolutely nothing!” I stand, finding it impossible to sit and yell at him. “Luca won’t tell me anything. He tried to hide the bruises from me. He pretended to be sick. Do you know that? He missed the last game of the hockey season. But maybe that was your point all along. Rough him up. Hurt him. Then, he can’t play hockey.”

“Watch your tone, and I don’t like what you’re insinuating, little girl.”

I huff and fold my arms across my chest.

“I’m not some little girl. I’m your son’s *wife*.”

“Precisely. You are only a part of this family because he married you out of protection.”

My gaze tightens.

“I love your son. Whether you see that or not, Luca is the world to me. Which is why I’m in here, demanding to know what the hell you’ve gotten him involved in!”

Dante straightens his back. His hands clasp the wooden desk in front of him. “That is none of your concern, Harper.”

“It is my concern when you send my husband home nearly beaten to death. I thought, as his father, you would have his best interests at heart, but you only care about your own self-preservation.”

My gaze darts across the office, not wanting to meet Dante’s stare any longer. My breath catches when I see the same gray dragon that Zeke has on his bed. Luca gifted it to him a few months ago.

But this one is damaged.

Ripped into with ... a knife of some sort.

The stitching and stuffing fluffs out with no attempt to fix. It’s shoved into the corner of the room against the wall, tucked next to the filing cabinet.

How peculiar.

Dante’s gaze sweeps over me, and when he catches me staring at the corner, he turns, glancing over his shoulder at the dragon.

I want to ask, but think better of it.

Was he angry with Zeke and took it out on the stuffed toy?

Why does he have the same toy that Zeke does? Did Luca have one as a child?

Or could it belong to the little boy who had been here last winter?

Dante is infuriating, and I pace the space in front of his desk. My mind is reeling with all the possibilities, and my silence might cause me more trouble. "I'm worried about Luca. I'm sure you can understand why I'm concerned, given what happened the last time he followed your orders."

"Luca is capable of handling the mission. In fact, he volunteered to be first in line today."

"What?" My voice catches in my throat. "No. I don't believe you."

Luca never wants anything to do with Dante. There's no way he offered up himself to get involved in a mission run and orchestrated by his father.

"Believe it." Dante doesn't so much as blink.

I don't know if the man has any tells, but I can't read

him. He'd be a great poker player, not a great opponent.

"Tell me what you're involving him in. Is it drugs? Weapons? Why is he willing to suddenly do your bidding? Did you threaten my son? Me?"

"You did that yourself when you went into that basement." Dante offers a sinister smile, and my stomach sinks. I stop pacing and fall back into the leather chair.

My head swims with regret all over again.

I bite down on my bottom lip, using the pain and strength to refocus as I glare across at Dante. I came in here demanding answers. I'm not about to stop now. If he had any leverage to hurt me, he'd have done it already.

He can't.

Because I'm married into the family.

A Ricci.

I jolt out of the chair and stare down at him. Towering above him makes me feel powerful, in control, and I notice a fancy blade, a dagger, on his desk. I reach for it before he has time to blink. "If

Luca won't tell me what the hell is going on, I expect you to give me answers, *Father*."

"It's *father-in-law* to you," he corrects me.

With the blade poised in my hand, I circle his desk, and Dante holds up his hands as he stands, forcing me to lose my leverage.

He's a hell of a lot taller and more intimidating when he's standing and we're face-to-face.

Dante grabs my wrist, yanking it upward so the tip grazes my neck. His strength overpowers me, and I'm forced to drop the hilt. The blade clanks to the floor.

His breath hits my ear, and I shiver. "Try that shit again, I dare you. Next time, I won't be as forgiving."

He pushes me backward.

I stumble a couple of steps, my heart pounding in my chest as I catch myself from falling.

"Sit." Dante points at the empty leather chair.

I'd rather leave, but it seems I've gotten my audience. I retreat to the chair, and he stalks around the desk, towering over me.

"What is it you want to know?" He perches himself on the edge of his desk, waiting for the barrage of questions.

"Tell me everything that Luca won't."

Dante smirks. "We'll be here all day, and I need to check on my son to make sure he hasn't gotten himself killed."

I launch up from the chair, and his hand comes to find my shoulder. "You should be seated for this." He pauses and strokes his jaw. "On second thought. Moreno!" he shouts.

It turns out he's standing on the opposite side of the door, waiting for Dante.

The door creaks open, and Moreno pokes his head into the office. "Yes, sir."

"Bring me Nikki."

Moreno shuts the door behind himself.

Dante's eyes bore into mine. "You will have your answers, but not until I'm satisfied."

"Satisfied?" I whisper.

What is he talking about?

A heaviness falls between us, and Nikki comes striding into the office. She glances from Dante to me, and her brow pinches. "What's going on?"

"Harper would like answers, and as much as I'd love to entertain the idea of giving her those answers, I need you to search her. Thoroughly."

"Excuse me?" My eyes widen, and I glance between the two of them.

"You could be wearing a wire." Dante gestures to my clothes. "Seeing as how I'm your father-in-law, I'm not getting my hands dirty with the search. Nikki, search her."

"Are you sure that's—"

"Search her," he bites out between clenched teeth.

"Got it. Would you give us some privacy?" Nikki escorts Dante out of his own office and shuts the door behind him.

She glances me over, perhaps waiting for me to undress. I don't budge an inch.

"Do I need to strip-search you, or can we do this like adults, and you fully undress for me?"

"I'm not taking my clothes off for you. I'm not taking my clothes off for anyone in this house other than my husband."

"Do you understand that if I'm not satisfied that you're not wearing a wire, then Dante will have his men do it?"

I lift my sweater, showing her my lace bra. "Satisfied?"

Nikki shakes her head and leans against the door. "All of it, off. And this isn't about satisfying me. I need to know you're to be trusted, and you haven't exactly exuded that level of confidence, have you?"

I scoff. "It was one time that I was snooping. Put it to rest."

"That would be easy if we could trust you. We've bent over backward for you and your son. Now, tell me what brought you into Dante's office."

"I want to know what's going on with Luca." I remove my sweater first, and Nikki holds a hand out, wanting to inspect each item of clothing.

"What do you mean? What's going on with my son?" Nikki asks.

When I'm down to my bra and panties, she makes me twirl around to ensure there's nothing on my back. "Bra and panties too. I've seen wires tucked inside them before."

Rolling my eyes, I remove my bra and undies, tossing both items at her. "Have fun."

She inspects it and then hands it back. Satisfied that I'm not wearing a wire, she hands me back my clothes. "Now, what is this about Luca?"

"The bruises. The cracked ribs. I want to know what's going on." I pull my clothes back on and her eyes tighten.

She had no idea about his injuries. "When did this happen?"

"Months ago, in the spring. He missed the last hockey game of the season because of his injuries."

I manage to slip on my pants, and I've barely gotten my arms through my sweater when Nikki barrels out into the hallway, facing her husband. I yank the hem down before anyone else can see my bra.

"What the hell did you get our son involved in?"

Nikki's steaming, and I'm glad to see that she's at least on my side.

Sort of.

"Relax." Dante puts his hands on Nikki's shoulders. His voice is calm, but it doesn't do anything to soothe my nerves.

"Don't tell me to *relax.*" She shoves his hands away. "What the hell did you get our son involved with? What did you have him go and do?"

He gestures for Nikki to step into his office.

Is he about to kick me out?

"Any wires? Bugs? Listening devices?" Dante asks, glancing me over.

"She's clean. What is going on with Luca?" Nikki glowers at her husband, and for the first time, I'm not sure who actually has more power.

It's an interesting combination to see. She clearly doesn't take orders from him.

"Your brother is back in the picture."

Nikki's eyes widen. "Massimo?" She steps backward

into the desk, and Dante guides her to sit in his chair.

I watch with fascination how he treats her, like a queen.

"Why didn't you tell me?" Nikki seems to forget that I'm in the room, or maybe she doesn't care.

"I didn't think you wanted to know." Dante's eyes flinch, and I suspect he's lying.

"You didn't want me to know." Nikki shakes her head. "How does this have anything to do with our son?"

"I wasn't sure who was behind the smuggling operation. I had my suspicions it was tied to the DeLucas, but I wasn't expecting it to be your brother."

"Once you found out it was, you should have come to me!" Nikki stands and heads for the door.

Dante is right there, blocking her way, pulling her into his arms.

Manipulative savage.

"We only know it's Massimo because of Luca."

She huffs and untangles from his embrace. "That doesn't make me feel better."

I sit at the edge of the leather chair, engrossed, and surprised Dante hasn't kicked me out of his office.

He probably forgot about me, or rather, I'm a minuscule problem compared to his wife.

"You know I always send teams out in pairs. Ashton and Luca did a little surveillance work; it just ... got dicey."

"What does that even mean?" Nikki steps forward, invading Dante's personal space.

He's silent, choosing not to speak.

Nikki answers for him. "It means Luca came home with bruises on his chest and broken ribs last spring."

"I gave him time to heal." Dante offers a smile.

"That's why my son hasn't been here all summer? And here I thought you were actually letting him spend some time with his family!" She smacks his arm. "Jerk. You never should have lied to me."

Dante runs his hands up and down Nikki's arms, attempting to soothe her. "I didn't lie, kitten, I just refrained from sharing the whole story with you."

"Same fucking difference," she bites out. "Where is our son now?"

Dante glances from Nikki to me. "This time, I sent Luca and Ashton with Halsey and his team."

"Wait—" Nikki holds up a hand. "You sent the boys on their own last time? What the hell were you thinking? Were you trying to get my son killed?"

"He's *our* son," he bites out defensively.

"And you still put him in danger!" Nikki's fuming and her cheeks redden.

Dante looks a bit uncomfortable. "I was thinking that they wouldn't be recognizable and would keep a safe distance. Clearly, I was wrong. I won't make that mistake again."

"Damn right, you won't. If you're expecting our son to take over the family business one day, you'd better make sure to keep him alive." Nikki smacks his arm again and then retreats back to his leather chair.

Dante watches her closely, smiling. There's a hum of electricity in the room, a heat sizzling between the two of them.

Nikki glances up at me. It's the first time she's paid me any attention since she had me strip down to nothing. "Harper, you're dismissed."

The way Nikki commands the room from Dante's chair, it's hard not to believe she isn't the one in charge.

My lips part, and I sigh. I appreciate what I've learned, but I'm still not confident about what's going on with Luca and that he's safe.

I stand from my seat but don't move toward the door. "What is my husband involved in?"

Dante glances at me over his shoulder. "My wife gave you an order."

"And I came in here for answers about Luca."

"We've told you all that you're going to hear." Dante points at the door.

"You made me strip down to tell me that her brother, Massimo, is behind whatever the hell is happening?" I laugh darkly, the absurdity of it burns me.

Did they just play me?

Dante approaches the office door and yanks it open. “You’re dismissed, Harper.”

I glance back at Nikki, desperately hoping that she’ll help. She raises an eyebrow. “You heard him.”

I curse under my breath and stomp out of the office. But I’m wearing socks, and my heavy footfalls on marble fall silent.

EIGHTEEN

NIKKI

"You surprise me, love." I tilt my head, gesturing for him to come closer with one finger.

Dante secures the office door and lifts me out of his chair, planting my ass on the edge of his desk.

He nudges my knees apart, standing between them.

"How is that?" he whispers against my neck, his breath tickling my skin before kissing a warm trail behind my ear.

"You continue to scare Harper, all the while playing the two of us." I yank on Dante's tie and bring his mouth to mine.

I don't kiss him.

"You didn't tell me everything while she was in here. What did you leave out?"

I wait for Dante to explain everything.

Already, from Harper, I know that my son had his ribs smashed in, from my brother or his men. Same difference.

Dante has failed to mention that my son was injured on the job. I had to bring it up. What else is he hiding from me?

His lips hover over mine. "Nothing of importance, kitten."

He leans closer, and I scoot backward on the desk. "You can't lie to me. I can just go ask Moreno. He will be truthful if you won't."

Dante's eyes glower, and he pulls back, glancing up at the ceiling.

I know how to get under his skin.

"Moreno is my second in command. He answers to *me*." His tongue darts out, grazing the corner of his lips. It's something he does when he's deep in thought and holding back from me.

I cross my legs, my feet pushing him farther away.

"Were you going to tell me that my son was assaulted on one of *your* missions?" I snarl at him. "It's been months since the attack. You should have told me the truth!"

"Why? So, you would worry that Massimo is out there, threatening our family? I'm taking care of it."

Wincing, I shake my head. "I know that look. You're leaving something out."

Dante is silent for a long moment.

It stretches onward.

Is he really not going to answer me?

I climb off the desk and saunter toward the office door.

He grabs my wrist, pulling me back into his arms. "Where do you think you're going, kitten?"

"To get answers. If you're not going to give them to me, your men will." I tug out of his grasp, but his hands fall to my waist, his touch warm, sensual.

I've been married long enough to know what he's trying to do—distract me.

Dante may be their superior, but they fear me almost as much as they fear him. There isn't much they keep from me, and whatever he's hiding will come out.

"Massimo threatened Harper and Zeke. When Luca was assaulted at the cabin, he made a vow to tear apart the family."

I back away, stumbling into the door. By the look on Dante's face, he's said everything that he's kept silent about for months.

"He must be stopped." My eyes glisten just thinking about that little boy, Zeke.

"It's already been set into motion. Relax, kitten. I have it handled. Harper and Zeke are safe under our roof. We have two of the strongest men here to protect the family." He's referring to Moreno and himself.

It makes sense why Moreno stayed behind. Quite often, he's leading the charge, with the capo following his orders.

"You sent our son to stop Massimo. He'll get himself killed!"

Luca should have remained here as well, protecting his family, not fighting for ours. I storm out of the office and run into Moreno, who has the phone to his ear.

"Is my son on that call?" I interrupt, not caring that he ranks well above me.

I don't follow the mafia chain of command.

Moreno's gaze tightens on me. He covers the mouthpiece. "It's Halsey, giving me an update. Would you like me to relay a message to Luca for you?"

"Tell Halsey if anything happens to my boy, he's dead."

"Nikki," Dante's voice is enchanting, but it doesn't work on me. "Come back to the office. Let's *talk*."

I sway my hips, wandering to the stairs, and Dante hurries out of the office and pounces on me, not even letting me make it up the steps. He pulls me around to face him, his arms tightly wrapped around my body, keeping me from moving.

"You're a fucking wild child."

I smirk, well aware of what ticks him off. "What are you going to do about it?"

He growls and kisses me before throwing me over his shoulder and carrying me up two flights of stairs.

I'm surprised we make it to the hallway, but we don't make it into the bedroom.

His mouth is on my neck, his fingers tearing at my clothes, desperate, frenzied, and fueled with passion.

NINETEEN

LUCA

We ride in three vehicles of Dante's, to the location on the map. Ashton and I ride together, but Halsey is the one who drives.

"Luca, there's a set of blades in the back, under the seat, grab those for me, would you?"

"Sure." I'm not sure what he intends to do with them, but I retrieve a black leather box with a snap latch that I open.

"Each of you grab two. Put them along the edge of your boots. I've got guns in the backseat as well. Take whatever you think you'll need. This could get messy."

The daggers are quite stunning, and I slide them carefully down into my boot, making sure they're secure.

Ashton grabs two as well and glances at them for a moment. "Are these necessary? I'm better with a gun."

"You're better off *alive.*" Halsey keeps his hands on the steering wheel as he follows his team; we're the last in position on our approach. "Don't ever turn down a weapon."

We're not quiet or secretive.

There's no sneaking up on the enemy. Once again, we don't have the element of surprise. Daylight doesn't exactly help, either.

In fact, there has been nothing for miles while driving, and there doesn't appear to be much nearby.

Four white vans spread across the forest road, which widens only slightly, the path trampled and clearly used before.

Each van is parked alongside one another, lined up, extending onto the forest floor.

We block their vehicles, pulling in behind the vans, lining up, making sure they can't drive down the mountain without going through us first.

The van closest to us has the back door open, and the young girls—teenagers—are being shoved inside like cattle, by two men.

In the distance, there's another road that winds up the mountain, and while we're the only path down, I spot a dark red shipping container, the doors open.

Is that where the girls had been kept?

There's no sign of anyone else coming from that direction.

Two men and all those girls.

We can overpower them and stop this before it becomes a bloodbath and the girls get hurt.

Anger floods my senses. Nausea sweeps over my body, and I jump out of the SUV first, needing air.

Hasley and the others are out of the vehicles within seconds, guns drawn.

The mountains make it less hot, the canopy from the

trees offering little comfort as I'm sweating and sick to my stomach.

Did Dante know?

I thought they were women being trafficked, adult women.

Not that it would make it much better, but the fact it's children, I can't see straight.

My heart pumps violently in my chest, each breath a gasp for air. The two men glance back at us, shove the girls into the van more quickly and raise their weapons.

There's no sign of Massimo, the man who threatened my wife and son.

He's the one I want dead most of all, but the men who are trafficking children, I have no problem with ending their pathetic lives.

The man on the right lifts his gun, and I duck behind the car door, using it as cover.

He's the first to pull the trigger.

Gunfire erupts all around, and within seconds, the

two men are splattered in blood and slump down, unconscious, to the ground.

They were no match for our team.

The van door is half-open, revealing the girls, but they don't move, frozen in fear or worried they'll be shot.

The silence lasts merely seconds as more gunfire erupts in the distance.

Bullets whiz by, one of them slamming into the metal door of the van, and the brunette girl nearest the door hides farther back inside the van with the others.

They're huddled together, terrified, cowering on the floor, afraid the bullets will penetrate the van.

So far, no one has shot the girls.

"We're here to help," I say, hoping they'll trust us. I offer my hand, but the nearest girl shakes her head, unwilling to step outside.

Ashton is right beside me, his gun drawn. "See if the keys are in the ignition." He shoots off a few rounds to keep us safe.

The van is parked beside the edge of a ravine. There's no one stupid enough to hide down the mountainside, which grants me the opportunity to use the van as cover as I sneak around to the driver's side door.

I try the doorknob and discover it's unlocked. Opening it, there's no sign of the van's keys.

Bullets shatter through the window, forcing me to duck for cover.

Shit.

"No keys," I shout at Ashton, hoping he has another brilliant plan, because this one isn't it. "Do you know how to hotwire a car?"

I catch sight through the window of the passenger door of two of Massimo's men moving in toward the van.

"Not while we're getting shot at. We need to retreat."

"Best idea I've heard all day," I mutter and back the fuck up to get more cover.

One door at the back of the dirty white van remains open, peppered with bullet holes, but it still provides decent enough cover to keep from getting shot.

At least they're not shooting at us while the girls are housed inside.

With our men shooting and momentarily gaining the upper hand, Halsey darts from behind the driver's side door of his car to the van with us.

I'm expecting him to rattle off orders.

He glances into the vehicle, his expression grim. "Shit, there are a lot of them." His gaze moves from the girls, slightly past the van's back door, to the three other awaiting vehicles used for trafficking girls. "This is bigger than we anticipated."

My mouth is dry. I don't like hearing that the capo in charge is feeling like we're not fully prepared for this fight.

"Please, help us," one of the girl's fragile voices echoes through the van.

Her voice reminds me of Harper, and it sends me reeling. We're here to put an end to the DeLuca empire that's risen and caused mayhem. Yet, I've seen no sign of the man behind the trafficking ring.

"Where the hell is Massimo?"

"If you find him, kill the bastard for me." Halsey fires several more rounds before taking cover and changing the clip on his gun.

More gunfire fills the air, bullets hitting the van, and screams erupt from the girls as they cower and huddle together.

Their tears and cries for help are gut-wrenching.

How dare Massimo prey on innocent children, little girls, to run his sickening business.

"Stay down, don't move," I order, trying to keep the girls alive.

Boots stomp over the earth, the sound of leaves and branches breaking, like a thunderous applause heading our way. It's not one or two foot soldiers, but dozens of them waging war.

We're overpowered, once again.

I don't see where they're coming from. There must be a base or some type of foothold they have nearby. Could it be just beyond the shipping container?

Bullets ricochet and blood scrapes at the girl's skin as bullets spray everywhere from the frontline, hitting all four vans wildly and without abandon.

There's no control or precision to their attack.

Alessandro, one of Halsey's soldiers, shoots from behind the farthest van, and a spray of bullets charges at him.

He's pinned down, but he's trying to draw the men away from the girls.

He's going to get himself killed.

"Cover me." Ashton doesn't even give me time to answer as he darts out from behind the van's back door toward the next awaiting vehicle.

Halsey and the team shoot at the enemy, giving Ashton enough time to run without getting hit.

It's a dangerous tactic, and I can't help but wonder what he's planning.

He tries the back door of another van, but it's locked. "Anyone inside?" He hits the door with his fist.

I can't hear anything over the sound of bullets, but I glance at Ashton from around the back of the van's door, making sure not to be seen.

He's gesturing and nodding, making it clear that there are more girls inside the second van.

"We need to draw DeLuca's men away from the vehicles."

"We do that, and we're all as good as dead." Halsey shakes his head, not in agreement.

If we can't drive off with the vehicles, then we need to disable them and keep the girls on the property. It's the best chance we have of stopping them from being moved.

I bend down and retrieve the blade tucked into my boot.

"Cover me." I work on the vehicle I'm closest to, ripping the back two tires, shredding into the rubber with the dagger.

I stay out of sight, slicing the front driver's side tire. It's the best I can do, three out of four without being a target myself.

I retreat behind the vehicle, the men never noticing me as they're shooting at Alessandro.

He's still pinned down but alive.

Bruno has skirted around the vehicles and deeper into the woods, taking out men as quickly as he can, unseen. He picks them off, one at a time, and his movements are quiet and swift, constantly changing, making sure he himself isn't a target.

Ashton and Alessandro notice what I've done with the vehicle, and they both slash the back tires of the vans in front of them.

It'll slow down the men if they try to leave, but it does nothing to stop the assault of bullets on us.

I've yet to fire the gun Halsey gave me. There are too many men shooting as soon as I glance around the edge of the vehicle.

Fuck.

Dante's men are trained for this type of assault.

Behind Halsey, I catch sight of a man in a suit fleeing on foot. I don't see who it is, but the attire, the fact he's fleeing, makes my skin crawl.

My insides scream that it's Massimo.

The man darts into the woods, and I dash between the vehicles, bullets firing, and I swear I feel the heat of one graze me.

There's no pain.

And whether it's adrenaline or a close call, I don't have time to slow down and check myself over to see if I've been shot.

The assailant runs down the mountainside, and I'm tearing up the ground, chasing after him, catching up.

I'm faster, but the mountain is steep and unforgiving.

Gunshots ring out above us, and the farther we get, the fainter they sound, but there are not any less.

Hopefully, our men are holding their position if not overtaking them.

It's too difficult for me to shoot a moving target, and I can't aim while running. My best option is to catch the bastard who fled.

I lunge at him, tackling the man to the ground, my fist pummeling his face.

His chest erupts in laughter.

It's dark.

Seedy.

He turns his head slightly, so his face isn't shoved into the ground. "Do you really think you've won?"

That voice. It's impossible not to recognize it, as it haunts my dreams.

Massimo.

Of course, *he* ran.

He didn't want to wind up dead in the gunfight.

His men are disposable.

The girls probably are, as well, to him.

Disgusting.

I straddle his frame, landing blow after blow to his face.

Blood coats my knuckles and my clothes as I keep pounding the shit out of him.

"You threatened my family!" Another swing at his face.

Where is my fucking gun?

I had in when I was running and chasing him, but somewhere between lunging at him and pouncing on him, it's not in my grasp.

There are leaves and broken branches. Trees and

shadows dancing over the ground. There's no sight of my gun at first glance, but it could be anywhere.

Does Massimo have a weapon?

There isn't one on him that's noticeable to me, as I have him pinned under my weight, his face down in the dirt, his arms restrained behind his back.

There's another round of heavier gunfire above us, and then it settles to a quiet nothingness.

My stomach roils, not knowing if Ashton is still alive. If Dante's men won the fight or if, within seconds, Massimo's men will be tearing down the mountainside in search of their don, and I'll be the next one dead.

TWENTY

HARPER

There's something sinister going on under this roof.

Nova is playing a game on her phone, her attention barely on Zeke, but he's preoccupied in the playroom with the train set, which seems to fascinate him.

I've been leaning on the wall, with a vantage point of Dante's office.

I need to get that stuffed dragon.

Zeke has the same one at home.

The same color.

The same size.

I wouldn't have thought anything of it, except for the way it had been violently torn into, the face of the dragon ripped apart.

Had it belonged to the child in the basement?

I know Luca told me that everything is fine. The child is safe, but how can that little boy ever be safe if the mafia murdered his family?

Shouldn't they pay for what they've done?

Had they destroyed his stuffed dragon, his favorite toy, as a threat?

Nova doesn't pay me any attention, and I head out of the office when I watch Dante carry Nikki up the stairs.

There are less of Dante's men here than usual. Hopefully, no one is paying attention to me because they're too busy doing whatever it is they do all day.

I hurry to Dante's office and give a pretend knock.

If anyone watches the feed and isn't aware that Dante has snuck upstairs with his wife, then maybe they'll think he's in the office.

I step inside, closing the door behind myself.

At least there are no cameras inside his office.

I hurry across the room and grab the stuffed dragon. On further inspection, it looks like a knife was the culprit.

The dagger that was on the desk earlier isn't left on display. I try the desk drawer, but it's locked.

I tuck the stuffed toy under the crook of my arm and hurry out of Dante's office and back toward the playroom. "Zeke, would you like to go to the park?"

I won't leave my son behind with monsters.

While I trust Nova with Zeke, I don't trust Dante and Nikki alone with him.

"Yes!" he squeals and runs right for me.

Nova glances up from her phone. "We should let them know where we're heading."

"I already told them."

It's an easy lie, and I force a smile. "You can hang back here if you want some quiet time."

“You don’t mind?” Nova meets my stare for a fraction of a second.

“Not at all. We’ll be back in an hour. Two, max. I’m going to take Luca’s car.”

“Okay. I’ll see you in a bit. Have fun.”

I slip on Zeke’s shoes and then mine. I keep the dragon tucked under my arm and head out to the car, buckling Zeke into the backseat.

“Mama, my dragon.” Zeke points at the stuffed animal, which I had tucked the head under my arm so he couldn’t quite see the damage done to the toy.

No sense in upsetting him.

“How about you count everything red that you see outside the window?” I ask, distracting him. He’s been working on learning to count.

He nods vigorously. I strap him into his car seat, shut the door and climb into the front seat, putting the stuffed dragon in the passenger seat up front with me.

I’m relieved Nova didn’t insist on tagging along. I pull the car to the gate and press the buzzer to exit.

The intercom buzzes, and immediately, a gruff voice I don't quite recognize crackles through the system.

"Where are you going?"

It doesn't sound like Dante, but it could be him. The voice is a bit muffled through the intercom.

"I'm taking Zeke to the park, and then we might get a snack since it's hot outside." I don't want to say the word *ice cream* and then not deliver it. He'll be devastated.

That seems to satisfy the man on the other end of the intercom, and he buzzes me off the property.

The gates open slowly, and once they're parted, I turn left toward the park before backtracking on another road away from the house, to head in the direction of the police station.

"Mama, you drive funny," Zeke says, and I glance at him in the rearview mirror.

"Are you counting red, buddy?"

"One. Two."

Ten minutes later, I pull up outside the police station, unbuckle Zeke and carry him inside. On one hip, I have Zeke, in my other hand, the torn stuffed dragon. I try to keep it out of Zeke's reach and his line of sight, because the moment he sees it, I fear what will happen.

There's a male officer in his fifties seated behind the front desk. He glances me over, noticing I'm carrying Zeke, and offers a polite nod. "Can I help you?"

My breath catches in my throat.

Am I nervous?

I'm terrified.

But fear can't control me.

Dante is a monster.

He kidnapped a little boy and murdered an entire family.

He must be stopped.

To protect my son and family, I have no choice but to take down Dante Ricci.

To Be Continued...

Continue the story in Between Steel and Secrets (Crimson Ice Book 5) available from Willow Fox.

Betrayal runs deep inside the mafia, and those who seek to escape or spill secrets may also spill blood.

Luca would do anything to protect his family…

Including keeping secrets from Harper,

Because the most dangerous secret could get him locked up behind bars…

Working for the mafia isn't just deadly, it's criminal.

Liam and Bristol have a tempestuous past…

They hate each other.

And their first date was no different.

But that undeniable spark is still there…

Even though they attend different universities, they happen to cross paths, and when they do…

Liam has the chance to become Bristol's hero or the villain in her story.

As a child of the mafia, which path will he take?

SHOP SIGNED AND EXCLUSIVE EDITIONS

THANK you so much for reading Between Sin and Silence. I hope you enjoyed the novel. Be sure to sign up for my newsletter for up-to-date new release details, sales, early release news, and more!

If you love signed paperbacks, special edition books, or discounted book bundles be sure to check out my online bookshop: https://shopwillowfox.com

ABOUT THE AUTHOR

Willow Fox has written in multiple genres. She's written everything from young adult dystopian to spicy RomCom novels. Her books have been translated into five languages and sold across the world.

Whether Willow is writing romance or sitting outside by the bonfire reading a good book, she loves the magic of the written word.

Follow her on any of her social media sites or through her newsletter!

Willow also writes kinky romance books under the pen name Allison West.

Visit her website at:

shopwillowfox.com

ALSO BY WILLOW FOX

Eagle Tactical Series

Expose: Jaxson

Stealth: Mason

Conceal: Lincoln

Covert: Jayden

Truce: Declan

Mafia Marriages

Secret Vow

Captive Vow

Savage Vow

Unwilling Vow

Ruthless Vow

Bratva Brothers

Brutal Boss

Wicked Boss

Possessive Boss

Obsessive Boss

Dangerous Boss

Bossy Single Dad Series

Billionaire Grump

Mountain Grump

Bachelor Grump

Ice Dragons Hockey Romance

Faking it with the Billionaire

Daring the Hockey Player

Arresting the Hockey Player

Crimson Ice

Between Blades and Blood

Between Ice and Oaths

Between Fire and Frost

Between Sin and Silence

Between Steel and Secrets

Between Storms and Scars

Want more kinky romance? I also write under the pen name Allison West.

Gem Apocalypse Series

Emerald Rebellion

Amber Voyeur

Sapphire Sacrifice

Scarlet Assassin

Crimson Crown

Royally Claimed Series

Palace Secrets

Maiden Claimed

Grave Misfortune

Academy of Littles

Little Etta

Little Gigi

Little Eliza

Reforming the Rebellious

Little Lizzie's Reform (Little Lizzie)

Little Prim and Proper (Little Kat)

Virtue and Vice

A Proper Punishment (Little Lena)

Little Brides (Little Clara)

Dowries and Deception

Delia's Debt (Little Delia)

Decoy Bride (Little Vera)

Jessie's Secret

Violet's Penance

Piper's Escape

Fiery Luna

Little Jade

Little Alice

Little Love Bundle/Western Daddies

Little Samantha

Little Lexa

Little Autumn

Little Rosie

Prefer a sweeter romance with action and adventure? Check out these titles under the name Ruth Silver.

Aberrant Series

Love Forbidden

Secrets Forbidden

Magic Forbidden

Escape Forbidden

Refuge Forbidden

Nightblood

Royal Reaper

Stolen Art